THE

HAUNTED PLACES BOOK 6

Boris Bacic

Every once in a while, we become ships lost in the storm—and someone becomes our lighthouse.

Contents

The Vanishing of the Lighthouse Keeper 7

Prologue 9

Chapter 1 15

Chapter 2 21

Chapter 3 29

Chapter 4 36

Chapter 5 44

Chapter 6 57

Chapter 7 65

Chapter 8 76

Chapter 9 86

Chapter 10 94

Chapter 11 98

Chapter 12 108

Chapter 13 117

Chapter 14 127

Chapter 15 136

Chapter 16 142

Chapter 17 150

Chapter 18 161

Chapter 19 165

Chapter 20 175

Chapter 21 182

Chapter 22 188

Epilogue.. 197

About the Author 200

Final Notes... 202

More From The Author...................................... 204

THE VANISHING OF THE LIGHTHOUSE KEEPER

The official story differed on each occasion. Some believed that the lighthouse keeper had come from a deeply troubled life, looking for an escape. After being unable to cope with the problems that haunted him, he climbed the dome of the lighthouse and threw himself into the ocean.

Others believed that he was swallowed by the tall waves on a stormy night.

Neither of those theories explained the keeper's disappearance, though. What was even more puzzling was the diary he had left behind.

In it, he wrote about a terrible storm and colossal waves that made him pray for his life. The keeper was perfectly safe from the waves inside the lighthouse, and he should have known that, and yet for some reason, he was terrified.

Over the next few days, he wrote about the storm raging, and then finally calming down. Eventually, no answers about his whereabouts were ever found, and the suicide story became the widely accepted one, mostly because of the last sentence he had written in his diary.

It's so peaceful out here.

After his death, the lighthouse had become known as haunted, but only among the crew working there, in order to prevent prying eyes from visiting.

The people stationed there reported witnessing various strange occurrences: footsteps upstairs, whispers in the night, the radio crackling with an unfamiliar voice for split seconds, and on certain nights—and this was the rarest of them all—at exactly 11:30 p.m., visages of a figure standing on the dome as if ready to leap off the lighthouse and into the violent waves below.

The lantern would sweep across, clearly illuminating the dead lighthouse keeper, and the next time it rotated…

He would be gone, just like that, leaving the witness to decide whether it was real or not.

PROLOGUE

Jeremy was awake long before the alarm clock rang. His screaming bladder had woken him up while it was still dark. By the time he was done using the bathroom, he found that keeping his eyes open was easier than closing them. He spent the next few hours tossing and turning. He was in the state of being tired but unable to fall asleep.

Eventually, his gaze shifted toward the window as he waited for daylight to chase away the darkness. He'd contemplated getting up before the alarm clock and starting his day early but ended up trying to get some shuteye instead.

By the time the obnoxious thing started blaring, his eyelids had grown heavy again. That was how things always went. Sleep wouldn't come in the quiet hours of the night. Nope, that was when the thoughts took over. Instead, sleepiness would come just before the alarm was supposed to wake him up. That was when the call of the dreamland was the most alluring; the most potent.

Jeremy yanked the covers off and swung his legs off the edge of the bed. The clock's ringing sounded like it came from inside his skull. He slammed his palm on top of the thing to shut it up. Its *ring* let out a final, defiant echo before growing silent.

Groaning in annoyance, Jeremy rubbed his eyes and glanced at the window. The gray sky greeted him, relief slightly alleviating the dread from the nightmares that had plagued him. There was something about overcast weather that Jeremy preferred over the incessant rays of sunlight.

Ever since he was a little kid, he loved walking under the dark clouds. Perhaps it was because it gave him the feeling of waiting for something. Dark clouds meant rain would start soon, and maybe that anticipation was what exhilarated him so much.

Jeremy stood up with a groan. The bedsprings squeaked as they dipped under his weight and leaped back up. A twinge of pain flashed through his knees, warning him not to make such sudden movements. He walked up to the chair where the pile of clothes from yesterday awaited him. After sniffing them to make sure they didn't stink too badly, he put on his cargo pants and sweater.

It was April, and the cold weather refused to abate, but Jeremy didn't mind. He preferred it over the scalding summers. Especially here. He pinched the blue beanie off the mound of clothes and stuffed it inside his pocket, just in case the wind was strong today.

After brushing his teeth, he went to the tiny kitchen to make some breakfast. Jeremy always ate eggs for breakfast, but he only had ten left. Enough to last him three more meals. There were canned goods in the house, sure, but Jeremy didn't like those much. Not that he ate regularly, but when he did, he at least tried to eat healthy enough to mitigate the adverse effects of his lifestyle.

His stomach rumbled when he cracked the two strips of bacon into the frying pan. The canned beans from last night had left him feeling unsatisfied, like eating half a meal and then having someone snatch the rest away.

After having his breakfast of three eggs, two strips of bacon, one piece of buttered toast, and a mug of coffee, he tossed the dirty dishes into the sink and ran some water on top of them to prevent the stains from latching on later. More plates waited to be washed under the newly joined one, but Jeremy couldn't deal with that at the moment. Right now, he had a job to do.

He snagged the keys from the rack on the foyer's wall, unlocked the front door, and stepped outside.

***

The cool breeze and the crashing of waves filled his ears the moment the door swung open. No need for the beanie yet. Jeremy stuffed the keys in his pocket, not bothering to lock the door. Not like anyone would traverse this barren strip of land and break into the house while he was gone working. He still locked the door at night just for his own self-assurance, but he reckoned there was no need for that, either. In the five months that he'd been stationed here, he hadn't seen a single person.

Not even a ship on the horizon.

His eyes flitted toward the thicket far across the grassy lands and then at the rocky pathway leading to the lighthouse. As he sauntered to the lighthouse, he took a mental note of what he needed to do for the day.

A day in the life of a lighthouse keeper was not very adventurous. Jeremy could finish his work in a matter of hours, and then he'd be free for the rest of the day. That's why he often took his time doing checkups and repairs, savoring every moment, getting lost in it.

This isolated place was one of the last remaining lighthouses in the world that wasn't automated. It wouldn't be long until it, too, was stripped of its human guardians in place of machinery. It occurred to Jeremy many times what luck it was that a job opening for a lighthouse keeper happened to be so close to his home.

After years of working in corporate, he couldn't imagine going back there, dealing with smug, rich bastards, trying to convince them why they should sign this deal or that. The pay was great, but the job itself was too stressful; too demanding. Jeremy often found himself, instead, prioritizing his work over family, and he hated that.

Here, he had his own peace and quiet. He didn't have a boss breathing down his neck because he didn't meet the quarterly quota. He didn't have to put in overtime to chase

11

a promotion that would give him more responsibility while keeping the same pay.

What would he do if he weren't a lighthouse keeper? The question ran through his mind many times, and the only other answer that came to him was: Fire Lookout. Lighthouse Keeper was better, though, as much as he disliked the rocky beach. There was a time when Jeremy loved spending nights in the woods. Camping, taking long hikes, or doing marathons.

Not anymore, though.

The pathway to the lighthouse was riddled with jagged, pointy rocks, which made it impossible for a leisurely stroll. Whenever he made his way to and from the lighthouse, hopping from one rock to the other, Jeremy stayed alert at all times. Once, his foot had slipped, and he had fallen sideways, and his hip slammed onto a sharp, protruding rock. It didn't puncture the skin, but it was enough to cause serious bruising.

It crossed his mind many times to carve a safe path, but the tools he was provided were not adequate for such a job. Perhaps he'd be able to chip away and make a path in months, but why bother going through such an ordeal and ruining his knees when he could do cardio every morning instead?

The waves grew significantly louder when he was halfway down the path. They lapped against the cliffside with a fierce intensity this morning, splashing the pathway. Jeremy knew that by the time he was back in the house, his sneakers and socks would be completely wet.

Sometimes, the ocean was so loud that Jeremy heard it reverberating all the way through the window of his bedroom at night. The noise had been annoying the first few nights, like a dripping tap, but then the waves became his lullaby—it was either the waves or the alcohol.

He was slightly winded by the time he reached the lighthouse. He would be out of breath by the time he arrived at the top.

Jeremy whipped out the keys and located the smallest one for the lighthouse door. He stuck it inside the keyhole, turned it, and pushed the door open.

CHAPTER 1

He squinted against the darkness of the interior, waiting for his eyes to adjust.

He then began the climb up the stairs.

Upon reaching the second floor, he fumbled for the light switch next to the door. The jaundiced light bathed the circular room serving as a bedroom. The lighthouse had been originally constructed with a bedroom and living quarters, but then the house off the shore was built to make the crew more comfortable, which pretty much caused the rooms in the lighthouse to fall into oblivion. But the rooms in the lighthouse weren't entirely forgotten.

Although Jeremy rarely spent time in the lighthouse's bedroom, the living quarters were where he kept his most personal belongings. He liked to separate his work space from his private space—an important lesson he was forced to learn at his previous job.

The bedroom was simplistic: an old bed, a nightstand where Jeremy kept all documents and photographs important to him, a wardrobe full of rubber boots and raincoats for those pesky stormy days when the waves were especially strong. Jeremy gave the room a once over before turning the lights off and moving to the next set of stairs.

His heavy breathing echoed in the entrapped space. By the time he was in front of the door on the third floor, he was panting. He swung open the door to the living quarters. His fingers fumbled along the wall until he located the light switch.

Unlike the bedroom where patinas of dust had already begun settling, the messiness of the living quarters made it clear that the room was often used—and by a slob like

Jeremy. A messy kitchen table, a rusted, portable stove, and a sink sat on one side of the room. A sofa, a coffee table, and an old TV occupied the other side. The TV, to Jeremy's knowledge, was broken, but he never bothered to give it a proper look.

Besides, the house had a TV and a DVD player of its own with an array of movies to choose from. Jeremy hadn't watched those. In fact, he had only turned on the TV twice. The first time was when he wanted to see if he could watch the regular programs (he couldn't). The second time was when he inserted some romantic comedy with Renée Zellweger into the DVD player. The interaction between the people in the movie reminded him too much of his old life.

The way he and Nadine had met.

The way they used to look at each other.

The promise of a future that was broken.

Jeremy had ended up muting the TV and leaning back in the sofa, his thoughts racing a million miles an hour. He had come to the lighthouse to escape. Not just to escape the world but the demons that plagued his mind. In a desperate attempt to salvage his broken sanity, Jeremy clutched the straw that was the job of a lighthouse keeper. He would be away from everything that caused him pain, everything that reminded him what a failure he was.

And it worked, but watching the movie had only triggered painful memories. That was the first time he had fallen asleep to the crashing waves outside.

The living quarters were stuffy. Jeremy hadn't noticed it until he tried to inhale and his throat constricted like being in a room full of smoke. He cranked open the window to feel a fresh whiff of air pleasant on his face. He then looked around the room. His eyes fell on the stacks of papers on the coffee table.

And the empty, overturned bottle of whiskey next to them. A brown droplet had fallen from the bottleneck on top of the paper. Jeremy squinted hard, trying to remember when he had drunk the bottle and how much he had actually drunk. It couldn't have been the entire bottle, right?

He thought back to three nights ago when he had last tasted alcohol. That must have been when he drank the entire bottle. But he didn't remember doing so, and that's what bothered him immensely. He stared intently at the bottle as if that would force it to yield some answers.

You're slipping, Jeremy. At this rate, I won't be able to save you, Doctor Martelle's voice entered his mind.

He shook his head, annoyed. He wasn't slipping. He was already too far gone.

He loped to the coffee table, bent down, and picked up the bottle, briefly glancing at the "14 DEAD IN SCHOOL SHOOTING, SUSPECT SHOT BY POLICE" headline of the newspaper article. He chucked the bottle into the trash can. The glass clinked against something in there. More bottles, he assumed, but convinced himself not to look out of fear of the pile he'd find.

His gaze fell on the floorboard under the sofa—the loose one where the lighthouse keepers kept all their stash. Six months ago, when Jeremy first arrived here, he was given a tour by his coworker, Matthew, and that included showing him the secret booze stash. Matthew was in his mid-twenties, and Jeremy could not, for the life of him, comprehend why anyone as perky as his coworker would subject himself to a job with such extreme isolation.

The area had no internet. The movies could only last so long. Books, too. Jeremy had already finished all the books he had hauled with him and was now in the process of rereading. He'd wanted to ask Matthew his reasons for accepting such a job, but then something told him that it wasn't his job to pry.

Matthew's demeanor radiated a contrasting energy to his outward exuberance. Something hidden far behind the veil of joviality that Jeremy recognized as sadness. Or was it pain? Or perhaps both?

If he had run into Matthew at the dollar store and seen his attitude, he wouldn't have given it a second thought. But nobody chose to be a lighthouse keeper because the pay was good or because it was fun. They did it because they craved solitude and an escape.

Just like Jeremy, Matthew was running away from something. An ex-girlfriend who had left him? Abusive parents? Jeremy tried not to linger on those thoughts. Matthew would be back to replace him in a month, and then it would be Jeremy's turn to return to the real world that he hated so much.

He winced at that. He'd gotten too used to the comfort and the serenity of the lighthouse, so much that he started seeing the place as his home. He hated the thought of being forced out of it for another lighthouse keeper to take over.

Normally, lighthouse keepers spent three months on each rotation, but Jeremy signed up for six, and with some tugging, he managed to convince the boss to allow him to stay for two rotations instead of one. But five months had already passed.

And they passed so quickly.

Maybe if you spent less time sobering up, you wouldn't feel like you fast-traveled through time, he reprimanded himself.

It was true. No matter how tranquil the lighthouse was, that quiet was exactly what he didn't need sometimes. In the darkness of the night, staring at the ceiling was when his brain would become the most active. It was when he would remember the most. It was when the urge to take a swig from the bottle was the strongest.

The more he ignored that thirst, the more it bothered him—like an itch just begging to be scratched. Most of the nights, he'd indulge. Not a lot. Just enough to help him fall asleep. But the problem was that the threshold kept moving. One drink turned into two, and when that wasn't enough, the quantity further increased until he began waking up with splitting headaches.

Maybe some time back in civilization will do me good. Maybe it'll help take my mind off things.

But even as he stared at the liquor stash, he didn't believe his own words. Jeremy forced himself to pry his gaze away from the booze stash under the sofa. He swung the door open and began ascending the spiral staircase toward the control room.

CHAPTER 2

The control room was where the communications devices were. It was where he informed the control tower once a day that everything was okay or asked for help if something went wrong. In the five months that he'd worked as a lighthouse keeper, his entire conversation with the control tower guy was whittled down to "Control, everything in check," and, "Roger that, lighthouse."

One would think that two people isolated in a lighthouse and a control tower would spend more time talking to each other to kill the boredom, but throughout his stay in the lighthouse, Jeremy had never heard the radio crackling to life unless it was to say, "Roger that, lighthouse." That was why he stopped carrying the portable radio with him ten days after starting the job, even though the rules stated that he should always have it with him. If an emergency arose (and Jeremy couldn't think of a single emergency, except for an impending hurricane, which was unlikely), then they could call him on his cellphone.

Jeremy pivoted around the control room, searching for any irregularities, and once he was sure that everything was in order (not counting the mess cluttering the room), he proceeded up the final set of stairs. By then, his lungs and thighs were burning from the exertion.

He had thought that it would be difficult climbing the stairs only for the first month or so. In fact, he was sure that going up and down the eighty-six steps once a day would be more than sufficient to mitigate the negative effects of bad eating and sleeping habits and a sedentary lifestyle.

Boy, was he wrong.

Climbing had become significantly easier since his arrival at the lighthouse, but it was nowhere close to what he thought it would be—effortlessly sprinting all the way up to the dome at the top in a single breath. Jeremy was forgetting a very important thing.

He was no longer in his twenties. The days when he could sprint across the entire football field without so much as raising his heart rate had long since passed. Now, even sitting for too long caused a pang to shoot through his lumbar back, jumping off things made his knees scream in protest, and he felt like a nap was constantly a blink away.

The dome of the lighthouse was, without a doubt, the most mesmerizing and terrifying sight in the entire area. Being so high up, Jeremy was able to overlook the thicket and the grasslands leading up to the lighthouse, and the ocean that stretched over the horizon.

The waves that weaved across the vast surface of the water looked calm from here, deceivingly so. He couldn't see it from here, but one glance down at the foaming water lapping against the rock formation that served as the foundation for the lighthouse would be enough to break that illusion. The waves were especially hypnotizing during stormy nights when they gyrated one after the other; colossal, destructive, but beautiful.

Jeremy climbed up to the lantern room daily only because he had to. If it were up to him, he would lock the door to the place and throw away the key.

Being so high up, surrounded by miles of prairies on one side and an infinite ocean on the other, Jeremy felt small. No, *tiny*. He was barely a grain of sand on a vast beach, just waiting to crash down into the earth.

The panes of glass surrounding the lantern room were dirty, smudged from the rain a few nights ago. He had promised himself that he would wash the windows in two days—and that was two days ago. Of all the duties he had at the lighthouse—and there weren't a lot of them—washing the windows was the one he hated the most.

Not just because he felt unsafe so high up but because it felt like an uphill battle. He would clean the windows, admire how sparkly they were, and then the droplets of rain would ruin his hard work. The same went with washing the dishes. He'd rid the sink of the dirty plates that had been sitting in it for days, make a meal, and the sink would magically fill up with more dirty dishes. He could finally understand why Nadine insisted so much on getting a dishwasher.

I didn't even realize how much time I spent cleaning the dishes every day until we got one of these, she had said a while after getting a dishwasher.

Dishwashers, robot vacuum cleaners, robot window cleaners... Who knows? In the future, we might end up getting all the chores done automatically by robots, Jeremy had told her flippantly, to which she agreed.

Jeremy looked toward the exterior of the lantern room. The railing looked far too low. He imagined a gust of wind blowing him right off the lighthouse, sending him plummeting to his inevitable death. Jeremy had never actively thought about that before he started working as a lighthouse keeper.

But ever since he started climbing up there daily, his gaze would inadvertently drift to the rocky bottom waiting far below, and then, sinister thoughts would plague his mind, whispering obscenities into his ear. He imagined leaping off the railing and crashing to the sharp rocks whose edges would eagerly greet him.

He wondered what it was like to commit suicide by jumping. And not just commit suicide but accidentally fall to one's death. What went on in their minds in those last seconds while they hurtled through the air, knowing there was nothing they could do to prevent their death?

That concept terrified Jeremy. It also prompted him to consider how he would kill himself if he were to do it. If he ever were to commit suicide, he would have chosen a less stressful way to do it. Swallow some pills, blow his brains out with a gun, hell, maybe even hang himself. But jumping off a high place?

No way in hell.

Those thoughts shouldn't even be in his mind. His will to stay alive had always been strong. Yet, he couldn't help but entertain them as of late; a morbid curiosity that somehow often found a way to wiggle itself into the back of his mind.

"Well, let's get you washed up," Jeremy said, his voice croaky.

His voice sounded strange even to him because it'd been so long since he'd said anything aloud aside from "Control, everything in check." He used to talk to himself all the time whenever he was home alone. Whether it be cutting up some vegetables or repairing something, he would talk to the inanimate objects as if they were real.

Well, time to cut you up, broccoli.

You're a stubborn door handle, aren't you?

He picked up the bucket full of dirty water from the last time and carried it all the way downstairs to the basement where the bathroom was. He emptied the bucket and rinsed it a few times before filling it with warm water. He huffed at the one hundred and two steps awaiting his climb to the dome.

***

Jeremy's shoulder was killing him by the time he reached the top floor again. Lugging a bucket full of water was difficult enough, but carrying one to the top of the lighthouse was far more challenging. He ended up sitting on the stairs twice to regain his breath before he reached the top.

Once there, he lowered the bucket onto the ground and wiped the sweat off his brow. *Yeah, now I remember why I hate doing this damn chore.* But as much as he hated it, the exertion also made him feel good. His body was warmed up, so his knees had stopped yelping, and the physical exercise made him feel like he was doing something productive.

The same could not be said for window washing.

Jeremy picked up some of the detergent from the floor and squeezed it into the bucket of water. He soaked the mop in the water and got to work. A few swipes down the glass were enough to determine that the windows were pretty much clean on the inside. It was the exterior that needed cleaning.

Shit. That was what he was afraid of.

A creak ripped through the top of the lighthouse. Jeremy gulped.

Just the wind.

His eyes shifted to the walkway outside. He licked his dry lips. His throat was constricted. He hadn't realized how clammy his hand was until he wiped it on his sweater.

You know well why you're afraid to go out there, Jer, a jeering voice snickered at him.

But then Doctor Martelle's words invaded his mind. *It's perfectly normal to develop phobias throughout adulthood, Jeremy. In fact, there are things that we are sure don't scare us until we come face to face with them. But differentiating rational fears from the irrational ones is what will help you deal with your phobias.*

Rational versus irrational fear, right. Easy. Okay. Irrational thoughts would be him slipping and somehow plummeting over the railing to his death. What about rational? Also slipping and falling over the railing to his death.

Coming to the decision to wash the window was easy. Climbing the lighthouse with the bucket in hand was also easy. But standing in front of the glass, contemplating going outside suddenly felt like a Herculean task.

For a moment, he wondered if it was even worth it to come out here. The windows weren't that dirty, were they? Why not leave it for Matthew to clean up? The kid would probably finish the job in a matter of minutes without giving it a second thought. Jeremy could imagine him whistling or humming while cleaning the windows as if it was no challenging task.

No. The windows had to be cleaned. And Jeremy had to be the one to clean them. When he'd applied for the job, the person interviewing him (if talking to someone while they're welding a piece of metal in a junkyard can even be considered an interview) had asked him if he had a fear of heights. Jeremy had brusquely shaken his head, and he'd meant it.

Back then, acrophobia meant nothing to him. It was just a word in the dictionary, no more powerful than the imaginary monsters that he'd spent nights chasing out of Ray's closet. No scarier than the story of the ghost haunting the lighthouse. But that was back then. Children were always brave during the daytime, but when night fell, they called to their parents to make sure there were no monsters around.

For Jeremy, the lantern room was stuck in perpetual nighttime, and the monsters he feared were real.

The windows had to be cleaned. It was his duty as a lighthouse keeper. Maybe he didn't need to wash all the windows. Just the dirty ones.

Jeremy shook his head, reprimanding himself for being such a scaredy-cat.

He picked up the bucket and mop, approached the door leading to the walkway outside, and squeezed the knob. With one slick twist, he swung the door open inward.

CHAPTER 3

The sounds of the ocean amplified. Jeremy squinted.

The sun had poked its head out of the clouds, casting annoying, warm rays on Jeremy. He took a tentative step forward, firmly planting his foot on the metallic floor. Even after cleaning the windows over ten times, his terrified mind couldn't help but imagine the floor collapsing and him falling along with the blocks of concrete.

He dragged the bucket outside and firmly gripped the mop. The sudden heat of the sun was relentless. Or perhaps, it was his own body temperature. To make matters worse, no shade was anywhere around the dome.

Jeremy looked up to see if any approaching clouds would perhaps grant him the mercy of shielding him from the yellow ball. A herd of gray clouds slinked across the sky, but it would be a while until they reached the sun.

Looking up made him dizzy. He averted his gaze down and clawed the air to find the wall for support, his balance gone. Once his fingers located it, he pressed his back against it for dear life. He vaguely became aware that he was in a half-crouching position. It wasn't enough. The urge to crawl on all fours overtook him, but he resisted it.

This was a terrible fucking idea.

Focusing on the rocky ground far below him did nothing to alleviate the sense of vertigo. The waves that licked the cliffs were like battering rams trying to topple the lighthouse. He knew in reality that such a thing was impossible, but what if it wasn't? What if the waves eroded the natural formation holding the lighthouse in place until the entire structure collapsed like a Jenga tower?

No, don't be stupid. That's impossible, you coward. Now, come on. Get cleaning!

But the part of him responsible for differentiating rational from the irrational was gone, no space left for it from the swelling panic that seized his every thought. Jeremy couldn't breathe. He allowed the mop to drop from his hand and then slid down the wall until he was in a sitting position, every inch of his backside pressed against the wall until it hurt.

Jeremy squeezed his eyes shut while his hands desperately fumbled for something to grab onto; something his fingers could close around just in case something tried to pull him off the lighthouse.

Just go back inside. You don't have to do this.

No, but he did. It wasn't just about the lighthouse duties anymore. It was about letting his fear control him like that. He could crawl back inside the lighthouse, yes. But what then? The shame he would feel over allowing his phobia to overpower him would burn stronger than the phobia itself.

Booze already had control over his life. He would be damned if he was going to surrender the reins to acrophobia, too.

Breathe, Jeremy. Breathe, Doctor Martelle's voice was clear as the wind that wobbled Jeremy.

He remembered the technique the doctor had told him about. Deep breaths. Inhale through the nose. Exhale through the mouth.

That's what he did.

At first, the breaths came as shallow hyperventilation. But after ten or so exhales, sucking in breath became easier even if just slightly. Jeremy opened his eyes.

That was a mistake.

His lungs refused to cooperate and take more than a strawful of air. His feet kicked to push himself farther into the wall. *Breathe, Jeremy.* Jeremy listened to the voice in his head. His eyes darted across the treetops, the vertigo still there but slowly abating. Only when his breathing calmed down did he realize how badly he was shaking.

His eyes flitted toward the mop soaking the floor. His fingers closed around the handle. He brought one knee closer and then the other. Planting a palm for support, he slowly began raising himself into a standing position. When his eyes fell on the grasslands that now seemed so far away (and so low down), he momentarily lost balance, which caused him to let out a yelp.

Breathe, Jeremy.

He didn't bother inhaling through his nose anymore. His breaths came out as erratic huffs like someone lifting a heavy object. And that was exactly what this ordeal felt like to him. Slowly, he straightened his legs until he was standing. His knees didn't like that, but their agony was only a distant whisper.

"Come on. Come on. Come on," Jeremy chanted, chiding himself for being such a coward.

It wasn't like he was standing on a tightrope suspended a hundred feet above the ground. He was on a walkway surrounded by a railing.

Yes, but it's at the top of a lighthouse.

Jeremy swung one foot over the other and then rotated until he was facing the lantern room windows. He resisted the urge to look at the clouds on the other side of the lighthouse. If he did so, he would realize how high he was and would lose his balance again.

Acrophobia? he'd asked Doctor Martelle once.

Yes. The fear of heights. Ever wonder why we get so dizzy when we're so high up, Jeremy?

Jeremy had shaken his head, waiting for an answer.

It's because when we're standing on a ground that's so high, but our eyes see another ground that's so low, the brain has trouble figuring out what information to trust. As a result, we may feel lightheaded or disoriented. It's like being seasick. You're inside a ship on firm ground, and the water outside is moving, and as a result, the overload of such information causes us to feel sick.

Cool, but how do you expect me to beat my phobias if even my brain can't process them properly? Jeremy had asked Doctor Martelle. The doctor had simply given him a courteous smile.

"Okay, come on," Jeremy said as he placed a palm on the glass and brought the mop as high up as he could.

Fingerprints on glass were the least of his worries. Not like anyone would see that. Once again, he resisted looking up out of fear of becoming lightheaded. After the first downward stroke, the second one came more easily. Then the third one.

Then Jeremy was sidling alongside the dome, one palm firmly on the glass, the tips of his sneakers digging into the wall, the mop steadily raking the glass, dispersing the mud and dirt on it. A few swipes later, dirty water soaked the mop, so it was time to dip it into water.

That was, perhaps, the most difficult part. Bending down to reach the bucket felt like doing gymnastics on the rings. Jeremy's entire body shook violently as he got down on one knee and lowered the mop into the water. This time, standing up was easier, and he moved along, cleaning the glass.

When he looked back to see how much progress he'd made, his heart sank. He wasn't even a quarter of a length done. To make matters worse, he completely forgot about the bucket, which was now a dozen feet or so away.

Goddammit.

He sidestepped back toward the bucket, grabbed the handle, and—

Standing up with it was not a good idea. As soon as the metallic container lifted off the floor, the world around Jeremy began spinning. He pressed his chest and face against the glass to stop himself from stumbling. When the image before him stopped wobbling, he dragged the bucket toward the dirty windows.

He sighed at the thought of how much more he had ahead of him. The muscles in his legs and arms burned. That reminded him to release his feverish grip on the glass, even if just a little. But as Jeremy continued cleaning the glass, the job became easier. Despite that, he transfixed his eyes on the lantern occupying the safety of the interior, not daring to look anywhere else.

See, Doc? I'm working on eliminating my fears, he thought to himself through clenched teeth.

Some of the mud clung persistently to the glass. Jeremy scrubbed hard, determined not to let a stupid lighthouse defeat him. How long had he been out there, wiping the windows? It felt like hours. The heat of the sun that only exacerbated his already profuse sweating told him that it couldn't have been more than ten, maybe fifteen minutes.

The relief that washed over him when he made it full circle back to the door was one he hadn't felt in a long time. He gave the windows one final, half-assed swipe and collapsed through the door. His back hitting the hard floor was the most beautiful thing in that moment.

The mop squeezed in his hand reminded him that the bucket was still outside. He didn't want to give himself too much time to breathe a sigh of relief. If he got cocooned in the overwhelming comfort that swaddled him, retrieving the bucket would become difficult.

He propped himself up into a sitting position, scooted toward the door, and outstretched a hand toward the bucket. His fingers brushed the metallic object, pushing it farther away. *Dammit.* Jeremy crawled closer to the threshold—closer to the edge that begged him to leap off—and his fingers closed around the rim of the bucket. He reeled it in, causing the water inside to slosh and drip onto the floor.

He couldn't get the thing inside fast enough. And once he did, he slammed the door shut so hard that the windows rattled. Silence took over. The wind that blew was shut out, along with the waves that constantly reminded him how far up he was.

Jeremy collapsed on his back, the cold sweat coating the sweater cooling his skin. He stared at the ceiling, his entire body still tense. Muscle by muscle, he relaxed: first his fingers, then arms and legs, then abdomen and back, then shoulders.

His body still shook as if suffering from a fever, but little by little, that abated just as his heart rate slowed down. Minutes passed, and Jeremy's eyelids became heavy. He felt like he could sleep for hours. He turned his head toward the closest window, giving it a middle finger in his mind.

He closed his eyes, not caring if he was going to fall asleep right there.

But then they shot open at a sound that caught his attention. Something downstairs.

A crackle followed by a tinny voice.

CHAPTER 4

Jeremy couldn't tell what the voice on the radio was saying. The few words that came through were punctuated by ensuing silence. Jeremy frowned, his gaze fixed on the ceiling, the pulsating of his heart reverberating in his ears.

He pushed himself into a standing position, a groan escaping his mouth. He blinked a few times, his head turning in the direction of the stairs. Another distinct crackle glided upstairs, followed by a murmur. Jeremy rubbed his eyes to stave off the sleepiness. He clambered up to his feet with great effort and lumbered toward the stairs.

His body felt like it weighed a ton, and all he wanted was to collapse in a soft bed and take a nap. As he descended the stairs, the radio fizzed to life again, the voice echoing inside the control room. Jeremy's steps slowed.

The voice that came through was feminine. The person who said, "Roger that, lighthouse," every day for the past five months was a male voice, so to suddenly hear someone else over the radio struck Jeremy as odd. He tried not to think anything of it as he descended into the control room.

He tip-toed down the final few steps, stopping on the last one, craning his neck to peek at the comms devices. The distinct *khhh* came from the communications desk, and then Jeremy heard the words of the voice clearly for the first time, "Hello? Anybody there?"

Another clipped *khh* sounded as the transmission ended. Jeremy held his breath. He knew full well that the person on the other side wouldn't be able to hear anything until he pressed the PTT button, but for some reason, he suddenly felt exposed.

It wasn't just that, either. It was the fact that something akin to dread clutched his chest. Ever since the fateful call he'd received five years ago, Jeremy dreaded receiving phone calls. Even hearing the doorbell ringing when he expected no guests was enough to send his panic skyrocketing.

"Whoever's in there, I need you to respond," the voice startled him, interrupting his train of thoughts.

Jeremy swallowed through a dry throat. His eyes fell on the window. He half-expected a face to stare back at him from there. Just the blue sky.

Pull yourself together, Jeremy.

He looked back at the radio. The feeling of being watched intensified.

The timbre of the voice communicated urgency, and everything inside Jeremy told him to run up to the radio and ask what was going on. But his mind reeled to find a logical explanation for the reason as to why the person on the other end—and a different person than the "Roger that, lighthouse" guy, at that—would be looking for the lighthouse keeper.

The first thought that came to his anxiety-riddled mind was: emergency. Something had happened, and they urgently needed him to respond. His brain just as quickly searched for all possible scenarios in which Jeremy would be needed for an emergency.

Maybe something about Nadine? No, probably not. So then, perhaps something about the lighthouse. Something important he had forgotten to take care of? Jeremy checked a mental checklist of the tasks and found far too few of them for him to forget any.

He stared at the radio on the desk, waiting for the voice to come from it again. He stopped in front of it, locked in a staring contest with the inanimate object.

"Hellooo? Are you alive in there?" the feminine voice asked in a sing-song voice.

Jeremy's shoulders drooped. The sense of urgency that the voice had conveyed earlier was gone. Whatever this was, it wasn't important. He then remembered that if it really was important, they would just call him on his cellphone.

He spun on the ball of his shoe to leave the room. He loped to the stairs, eager to put some distance between him and the radio. He barely took one step out of the room when the radio whirred to life again behind him, "If you don't respond soon, I'm going to have to contact HQ to send someone to check up on you."

Jeremy froze in his steps, a jolt of panic shooting through him. Having someone check up on him wasn't good. They'd determine he was okay, and that would raise questions about why he ignored the rules and didn't keep the radio on him at all times. He might even get fired.

Clenching his jaw, Jeremy turned to face the control room, his eyes falling on the blasted radio. A momentary thought occurred to him that he could just smash the radio into pieces and lie that he had an accident when they send someone.

But he didn't want anyone checking up on him. Why create such a hassle when there was probably no need for it? He sauntered to the radio and picked it up off the desk.

The woman's voice erupted from the speaker again, "Well, I'm just going to continue trying to reach you for now. If and when you hear my vo—"

"This is lighthouse. What's the emergency, Control?" Jeremy interrupted, his thumb firmly on the button.

Silence.

Jeremy inhaled through his nose, waiting for a response that never came. The lack of noise unnerved Jeremy more than the voice. A million thoughts swirled in his mind like tentacles groping to each get a piece of him.

What if the woman wasn't talking to him at all?

What if she wasn't from the control tower at all and just happened to be on this channel?

Before the paranoia could properly set in, the radio produced another loud *khhh*, and the woman's voice came forth. "Finally. I've been trying to reach you for a while now. Where have you been? Don't you know you're supposed to keep your radio on you at all times?"

The flurry of questions left Jeremy dumbfounded. He opened his mouth to respond, his thumb squeezing the PTT button, but no proper answer came to his mind. He let go of the button and closed his mouth.

"Did you disappear on me again?" the woman asked.

The panic that held on to Jeremy deflated, replaced by something he hadn't felt in a while.

Annoyance.

"No, I'm still here," he said.

More silence followed, and then she replied, "Okay. Why weren't you responding?"

Jeremy couldn't tell if the question was accusatory or curious.

"I was busy upstairs. Left the radio in the control room while I did some work."

"You're supposed to keep your radio on you at all times."

This time, the woman's tone sounded like an underpaid part-time worker quoting the rules she'd learned from her thirty-minute-long orientation.

"I'm aware of the rules, thank you." Jeremy scratched his forehead.

"All right," the woman said.

Jeremy held the radio up to his ear. Despite establishing that there was no emergency, he sensed that the conversation wasn't over. His assumption proved true a second later when the woman broke the silence again. "My name's Dannie, by the way. I'm new here."

He'd already figured it out somewhere along the way. Something about the woman's "Let's do everything by the book" tone was what gave her away.

Everyone was like that on their first day on the job. They followed all the rules, did everything exactly as the higher-ups meant for them to be done. But, little by little, they'd learn which rules had to be followed with stringent detail and which ones were utter bullshit.

Dannie would relax on her job after a while. She'd learn that there was no need to say anything past the daily "Roger that, lighthouse" exchange.

"You're still there, right?" Dannie asked.

Jeremy was free to ignore her, now that he knew there was no emergency. He was tempted to leave the radio on the desk without answering and go downstairs to continue work. He didn't know what compelled him to press the button on the radio and speak into it instead. "Yeah."

"So... want to tell me your name?" Dannie asked.

Jeremy hesitated for a moment. After deducing in his mind that there was no reason not to give this stranger his name, he said, "Jeremy."

"Jeremy," Dannie repeated as if testing the name on her tongue. "Well, nice to meet you, Jeremy."

Jeremy didn't respond. He didn't want to give her a reason to continue speaking. He just wanted the conversation over so that he could go back to work.

"So, how long have you been at the lighthouse, Jeremy?"

Jeremy gritted his teeth. He could already tell that Dannie was a talkative person; one who led the conversation most of the time, even when the other person gave one-word responses; one who continued talking when the person was late for their bus.

"Five months," Jeremy offered in a curt response.

His foot tapped on the floor as he waited for Dannie to say what she wanted to say so that he could drop the radio and leave. The communication strangely brought him back to the days when he used social media. Jeremy never was a patient enough person to stare at the screen while waiting for the three little dots hovering at the bottom of the chat to turn into a sentence from the other person. Oftentimes, he ended up disappearing mid-conversation.

He wondered if he could do the same with the radio.

"Did you say five months?" Dannie asked.

"Yeah."

"I thought lighthouse keepers were supposed to be stationed for three months only."

"Yeah. They are."

He didn't know why he thought he could end the conversation with such a terse answer.

"You're quite talkative, aren't you?" Dannie's voice was laced with a hint of amusement. When he didn't respond, she spoke up again. "So, I guess you're replacing someone? That's quite a favor to do for someone, isn't it?"

"Yeah. Listen, I have to get back to work." The words that came out of his mouth sounded a little too aloof, but it was too late to take them back. Besides, if having Dannie think he's an asshole would keep her from contacting him, then so be it.

"Right. I understand," she said.

Jeremy held on to the radio, expecting a follow-up to that. When the silence that draped the air went undisturbed for a while, he placed the radio back down, relieved that the interaction was over. He spun around when his exit was interrupted once again.

"Aren't you forgetting something, though?" Dannie's tinny voice came from the communications desk.

Jeremy turned around, his face contorting into a grimace. He raised a hand to his head, his nails raking his hair. He snatched the radio off the desk and pressed the button hard. "What?"

"You're supposed to keep the radio with you at all times."

CHAPTER 5

Jeremy wasn't happy about this new rule. He had spent five months in the lighthouse, away from the radio, and all of a sudden, this lady was telling him that he needed to keep it with him the entire time.

He didn't like the idea of someone being able to reach him at all times. That was why he'd ended up deleting his social media accounts in the first place.

He ran a hand down his face, thinking hard of a proper response to Dannie; something that would convince her that there was no need for such extreme measures.

"Are you still there, Jeremy? You're not ghosting me again, are you?" she asked.

The irritation that simmered in Jeremy's skull was reaching a crescendo. He clenched his jaw tightly to stave off the need to hurl the radio across the room. He took a deep breath to compose himself. "Yeah, I'm still here. Listen, there's no need for that. The guy who worked there before you... he and I only spoke once a day to break radio silence. There's nothing you need to worry about."

A smile tugged at the corners of his lips. The muscles in his cheeks hurt from the gesture, which prompted him to consider when the last time was that he'd smiled.

It was his well-rehearsed PR grin—the same one he'd flashed to new clients, day after day, while working in the corporate industry. The simplicity at which his muscle memory took over surprised him. It was as if the last time he'd brokered a deal was yesterday, and not two years ago.

The minuscule surge of confidence for thinking he still had it popped like a balloon at Dannie's next sentence. "Sorry, Jeremy. I've been given a list of strict rules, and they're right here in front of me on the wall. Here's what it says: If the lighthouse keeper fails to respond to your contact for more than six hours, inform HQ."

Jeremy let the air out of his lungs. He scratched the top of his head, the anger in his chest begging to be let out. A little devil sitting on his shoulder urged him to tell Dannie to fuck off with her rules and stomp the radio into smithereens.

But the voice of reason disagreed with that. Breaking the radio would only get Dannie to mount a rescue mission for Jeremy. When they arrived, they'd find him safe and sound. He'd explain that the radio was broken in an accident, and they would give him a new one. He wouldn't be able to get rid of the second one without the same results.

The fact that he was so powerless to stop this woman from dictating how he was going to spend his remaining time in the lighthouse made him want to ransack the entire room. Like it or not, she was in control, and if he wanted to keep his job, he would need to do exactly as she told him. It was like opening the front door to find a stranger with packed suitcases proclaiming, "Guess what? I live here now." And there was nothing Jeremy could do about it.

Okay, calm down. It's not so bad, he told himself.

He was right. It wasn't so bad. All he needed to do was keep the radio on him at all times. He would still only use it to inform Control that he was okay and then clip it back on his belt and let it sit there silently.

Was he happy about Dannie being able to speak to him any time she wanted? Absolutely not. And it didn't help that she was obviously such a talkative person. But Jeremy had a plan for that, too. Keep giving curt responses, and eventually, she would become bored and stop talking to him.

A flawless plan.

Jeremy stared at the radio in his hand. Although Dannie went quiet after citing the rules, he knew she was listening intently, waiting for his response. If he ignored her for long enough, she would realize that talking to him was like talking to a wall and would shut up.

"Okay," he simply said.

"You'll take the radio with you?" Dannie asked.

The silence between his final response and hers was brief, which confirmed that she had been waiting for him to acknowledge the rules.

"Yeah. I'll clip it on. But if I don't respond right away, it means I have my hands full, so don't go panicking and calling HQ."

"I won't go panicking. I worked as an EMT before this. I'm pretty level-headed, you know?"

EMT? Interesting.

Jeremy wondered what an EMT was doing working in a control tower relaying information from a lighthouse. Dannie didn't sound old enough to be retired. Perhaps she, too, was fed up with the shit she'd seen and needed some time away from the world.

"Right," Jeremy said. He felt like he should have said something else, but nothing came to his mind, so he let his finger slip off the button.

He stared at the communications device, waiting for Dannie to say something else, but it didn't happen. Jeremy let out a shaky breath, tentative relief enveloping him. Maybe having the radio on him at all times wouldn't be as bad as he made it out to be in his own head.

Irrational fears, Jeremy, Doctor Martelle snickered.

***

Sometime later, Jeremy was back in the lantern room. It had taken him a while to go all the way to the basement, empty the bucket of water, and then climb back up. He could have just emptied the dirty water into the ocean, but that would require going out onto the walkway around the dome and leaning over the railing, and he wasn't in the mood to brave his fears once more.

After setting the cleaning items aside, he turned the lantern on and tested whether the mechanisms worked properly. The blinding light forced his gaze to gravitate to the floor. The rotations worked perfectly, so he turned everything off.

The lantern was automated, but it was imperative to perform regular checkups from time to time. That meant changing the bad bulbs, oiling the hydraulics, and double-checking whether the automated devices located in the service room inside the house worked properly.

Although Jeremy wasn't an engineer, the boss was generous enough to leave him with a manual that he could follow if anything went wrong. Operating the complex machinery in charge of automating the lighthouse didn't seem too complicated since there weren't all that many buttons to play around with, but Jeremy was wary of touching anything electrical.

During his five months staying there, the lighthouse had only malfunctioned once—when the rotating system for the lantern stopped working. Following the step-by-step guide outlined in the tattered manual, Jeremy was able to restart it by flipping a switch off and on a few times.

Prior to arriving, he had been worried about not being able to fix things, especially since he was stranded in the middle of a deserted shore, but then the boss told him that he could contact Control any time he was having issues, and in the worst-case scenario, they would send a maintenance guy out to assist him.

Luckily, there had been no need for such a thing.

After making sure that the lantern functioned properly, Jeremy exited the lighthouse and closed the door. His eyes fell on the convergence of black clouds far off in the distance above the ocean. A storm was approaching.

He plodded across the rocky pathway leading back to the house, listening as the waves grew louder and more vicious; a warning from the upcoming storm.

Jeremy liked storms. There was something mesmerizing about being in a quiet house on a rainy night, listening to the tapping of the droplets hitting the roof. During such nights, Jeremy liked to dive into a book or stare at the window pelleted by the droplets of rain until he became sleepy. Add a little thunder into the mix, and it would make him feel better than any alcohol.

As he skipped from rock to rock, he couldn't help but become aware of the dead weight of the radio in his pocket. A part of him hoped that the thing would slip out and be swallowed by the water until he remembered that Dannie would contact HQ then.

Upon his return to the house, he entered the service room and began the weekly checkup of the machinery, meticulously following the manual. There were no strict rules on what days the checkup needed to be performed. It just needed to be done once a week.

Matthew had once told Jeremy that there was no need to stress so much over those things because they never caused any problems. When Jeremy told him he would rather be safe than sorry, Matthew suggested he do it on Sunday and Monday because then he'd have twelve days off. Jeremy offered a phantom smile and nodded his head, deciding, on the spot, that he would not do as Matthew suggested.

He was by no means a person who did everything to the letter as instructed. Some rules at a job could be ignored. But those were the minor rules like submitting a formal report to a twenty-year-old client who wasn't going to read it or showing up in the office on the day when there

48

were no scheduled meetings, or eating lunch at 12:30 instead of 1 p.m.

But checking on electronics that the entire lighthouse—and the living quarters of the keeper—depended on? That was a must-do in Jeremy's book.

"Hey. Are you still there?" the radio spoke from the workbench behind Jeremy.

His fingers were squeezing the manual in one hand. The other hand hovered above the green and red buttons and switches. When Dannie spoke up, she broke his focus, but he was determined to resume work. His eyes intermittently darted from the book to the buttons.

Okay, press this button here, and then this one. Then flip this up.

"Hello? Jeremy?"

Then this one here. And then... Jeremy stalled, making sure that he got the order right. *And then this big one here.*

His thumb sank into the big button on the side of the panel. Nothing happened.

"Shit," he cursed.

He must have gotten the sequence wrong. Now he would need to do the whole thing from scratch. Jeremy ran a hand through his hair.

"Jeremyyy? Hellooo?"

Jeremy plopped the manual on the workbench and brought the radio to his mouth. "What do you want? I'm working. I don't have time to entertain you if you're bored."

"Someone's a little snappy."

"I'm not snappy!" Jeremy bit down on his anger, realizing that the words came out too loud. "I'm not snappy. Look, don't you have work to do over there?"

"Nope. It's a quiet day."

"Okay. Well, I have a lot of work to do. So, if you don't mind..."

He waited for Dannie to get the hint.

"Oh, right. No, I totally understand."

Thank god.

"Just put me somewhere close, and I'll do the talking instead," Dannie finished.

Jeremy's radio hand drooped. He pressed his lips together in frustration and raised the radio back to his mouth, his finger hovering above the PTT button. He then decided not to say anything at all and, instead, hooked the radio to his pants before returning to the board. If Dannie talked, he would ignore her. He stared at the page of the manual, his hand tracing the buttons.

"So, what's wrong with you?" Dannie's question came so abruptly that Jeremy's gaze inadvertently wandered down to the radio.

The question was enigmatic enough to intrigue him, and he wondered if it was Dannie's intention all along. Jeremy was too focused on the board in front of him to give an apt response. He had made it too far into the button sequence to stop now. He flipped a switch up and down to reset the board. He pressed the first button then glanced back at the manual to make sure he got the right one.

He expected a wave of more questions on Dannie's end, but the only sound that accompanied him instead was the clacking of buttons that he pushed, one after another. His focus was elsewhere. Halfway through the button-pushing, he unclasped the radio and brought it to his mouth, unable to resist the urge. "What do you mean?"

Dannie's response came immediately, which told Jeremy that she'd been waiting like a predator ready to pounce its prey. "Come on, you know what I mean."

"What? Because I work in the lighthouse?" A huff escaped Jeremy's mouth.

"Not only that, but you've been there for five months."

"So?"

"So, I worked as dispatch for Concordia Station."

Jeremy frowned. "Where's that?"

"Concordia Station? You know? White Mars?"

Jeremy pressed the button and then let it go.

"Okay, you don't know about it," Dannie said. "Concordia Station is a research facility on the Antarctic Plateau. It's so isolated and surrounded by flatlands covered in snow that they dubbed it "White Mars." It's, like, five hundred miles away from any other place where humans live."

"The lighthouse can hardly compare to White Mars." Jeremy shook his head.

"Absolutely. But the people working there all share one thing in common."

"And what's that?"

"Everyone's running away from something."

Jeremy stared at the radio for a moment. "What makes you think that? Someone might just like the solitude."

He didn't know where the need to justify to Dannie came from.

"I can understand someone wanting some time alone. But what you do then is take a walk in the park, drive on a rarely used road, shut yourself in your room and blast loud music. After a couple of hours, you're back to being with people. But this kind of job? It's too extreme for so much time alone."

Jeremy clipped the radio back to his pants and continued pushing the buttons as instructed in the manual. His lack of response didn't stop Dannie from talking.

"Look. I worked as an EMT for ten years. Let me tell you something. Nights can get really boring there, but there's always someone to talk to, always something to do. At the end of the day, you get to go home. And then there's the anticipation of the call, never knowing when you'll need to rush out there to save someone's life. That

51

exhilaration makes up for the hours of yawning in the ambulance. EMTs are sort of adrenaline junkies. We love the rush, even though no one's going to admit it."

Jeremy pressed the big button to finish resetting the lighthouse automation systems. The top button blinked with a green color to indicate everything was in working order.

Finally.

He snatched the radio off his pants and said, "What's the point you're getting at?"

"The point I'm getting at is: EMTs—and all those jobs where you're waiting for something to happen—have something to look forward to, something to expect. But you, me, and the crew at Concordia Station? There's nothing for us. We're shutting ourselves away from the world in hopes of escaping our demons."

"Well, that's a very optimistic way to look at it." Jeremy sauntered out of the service room.

"I know, but it's the truth."

Dannie was right, but Jeremy didn't want to give her the satisfaction of admitting that her theory was correct. It didn't take a psychologist to understand that only the most broken people took up these kinds of jobs.

Jeremy had seen it in Matthew's eyes. No matter how hard he smiled, he couldn't hide the pain behind his eyes.

Just like Dannie. Beneath that perky voice were layers and layers of traumatic past experiences that shaped her into what she was today. The jovial attitude was her defense mechanism. It was there to take the attention away from the darkness that plagued her.

"I'm just a lighthouse keeper. No deeper secret to it," he finally said.

The lie sounded anything but convincing even to him.

"Right," Dannie's dry response came moments later.

He couldn't tell if she was being sarcastic, playing along, or if she actually bought his lie. Either way, he didn't care enough to ask her. He didn't feel like discussing such gloomy topics.

He opened the front door and stepped outside. The wind was much stronger now. With the sun gone behind the clouds once more, the cold started to take over. Jeremy hated how extreme the weather always got at the lighthouse. Either it was incessant rays of sunlight that burned him like a vampire or icy wind that flayed him from all sides.

"Hey, what kind of food do you guys have there?" Dannie asked, a bright contrast to the previous topic. "Because we mostly have non-perishable stuff here, like…"

But Jeremy wasn't listening. His eyes fell on the door of the lighthouse. It was open. Jeremy squinted against the wind at the gaping, rectangular maw at the bottom of the lighthouse. The wind was really strong today.

"Hold on," Jeremy interrupted the woman's food listing. "I need to check something."

"Oh, okay," Dannie said and then added something else, but Jeremy couldn't hear her over the gust of wind that crashed into him.

He put the radio into his pocket and hopped over the craggy pathway, his eyes flittering from the open door to the rocks he was stepping on. The radio crackled, Dannie's voice an imperceptible murmur. Whatever she wanted to say, it could wait.

The smell of salt in the air was intense. Jeremy had been acutely aware of it during the first few days of living at the lighthouse. Even after going back inside for the night, the salty redolence would cling to his lips and tongue. After a while, the smell just disappeared. It was probably still there, he figured, but his nostrils had grown accustomed to it.

Now that the approaching storm was splashing the waves around, the smell was more prominent. Jeremy's eyes sprang to the sky. The dark clouds on the horizon were moving fast, shrouding much of the previously celeste sky in a plethora of black and gray hues.

Jeremy hopped through the door of the lighthouse for shelter from the wind. From the inside, it whistled past the lighthouse and made the old structure groan. Something faintly clacked upstairs, and it wasn't until then that Jeremy remembered leaving a window open.

"Shit." He shut the door behind him, just barely silencing the raging winds.

"Jeremy? You're starting to worry me. Is everything okay?" Dannie's mechanical voice bounced off the walls.

Jeremy raced up the stairs. Something creaked somewhere. It gave him an uneasy feeling that the whole lighthouse was going to be blown out of the ground. He didn't let that dissuade him from doing his job as the keeper. He reached the bedroom, hearing the croaking and clacking on the floor above him louder now.

"Jeremy?" Dannie's voice persistently called to him.

He resisted the urge to chuck the radio across the room. He cursed himself for giving Dannie his name. Now he would need to suffer hearing it whenever he didn't respond for longer than a minute.

Serves you right for being a dumbass.

When he reached the living quarters, he stopped at the entrance, his eyes scanning the room. Papers flew all over the room. The window that he'd opened earlier swung open and then slammed shut with a loud bang. Jeremy winced at the house, hoping it didn't cause any damage to the glass.

Ignoring the bevy of papers scattered on the floor, he slogged across the room just as the wind blew the window open again. Jeremy's fingers took hold of the edge of the frame. He gently closed the window. The breeze outside slammed into the glass with a tap and whistle as if angry that the lighthouse keeper had stopped it from wreaking havoc.

His gaze fell to the scattered papers on the floor. Jeremy picked them up, one by one, and stacked them together. His eyes lingered on the last paper he picked up. 14 DEAD IN SCHOOL SHOOTING, SUSPECT SHOT BY POLICE glowered at him. Between the columns of text was a black and white photograph of a group of people hugging and crying.

Jeremy didn't know why he kept the newspaper. The urge to crumple it and toss it into the trash can overcame him. Before he could do so, the radio fizzed.

"Well, just respond when you have a minute," Dannie said, her voice now clear as the wind outside.

Jeremy pulled out the radio. "Yeah, I'm okay. Had to check something in the lighthouse."

"All right. Is everything okay over there?"

"Yeah. The wind is crazy, though. I guess it must have opened the lighthouse door."

"Yeah, I got word that there's a storm approaching. You should finish whatever you have and get back inside. It's going to be a wild one tonight."

Jeremy dropped the messily stacked papers onto the coffee table, giving the ominous newspaper headline a final glance before turning to climb farther up. He had to make sure all the other windows were closed before he settled in for the night. The last thing he wanted was to have to rush out of the house, across the rocks that would undoubtedly be slippery as hell, and into the lighthouse, to fix an issue that he overlooked during the day.

The lantern room gave him a better view outside. The gray sky was fury itself. The violent waves were ranks of soldiers charging into the onslaught. He grimaced at the fact that he unnecessarily went through the ordeal of washing the windows. He could have just let it rain and washed them at a later date. With this storm coming in, he would need to wash them at least once more before Matthew took over.

The thought of going back out there formed a knot in his stomach. He pushed those worries away, deciding he would care about them when the time came.

Jeremy twisted the knob of the door leading to the walkway and pulled it open a crack. He could feel the intensity of the wind pushing against his hold, trying to break in. He slammed the door back shut and locked it.

He then made his way down and checked every room along the way. Everything was in order.

By the time Jeremy had reached the bottom floor, the soft *tap-tap-tap* of the rain permeated the air. It was already starting.

Jeremy opened the door. The rain hadn't reached its full potency yet. A light drizzle showered the area, a warning of an impending storm. Jeremy shut the sturdy door behind him, locked it tight, and rushed across the traitorous pathway back to the house.

CHAPTER 6

The day had been a lot more eventful than Jeremy thought it would be. Not only did he need to brave the heights of the walkway to wash the windows, but he also had to get accustomed to a new rule. While carrying the radio with him was not really a new rule, it was new for him, and he didn't like sudden changes.

They made him anxious. Irritable. *Thirsty.*

While preparing mac and cheese in the kitchen, his eyes fell on one of the rarely used cupboards. He thought about opening it. He knew the heaven that awaited him there. Just one swig. It couldn't hurt to do that, right?

Yes, it could, a small voice in his head said.

He took a step closer to the cupboard and stared up at the small wooden handle that called to him. His arm automatically rose, his fingers inching toward the handle. Just open it and choose your poison. It was that easy.

Don't do it. Turn around and forget about it, the small voice urged him, but it was much quieter, much more timid than the one nudging him toward the alcohol.

The tremor in his hand was violent with anticipation of the treat he was about to give himself. His fingers feverishly closed around the tiny handle. He pulled it, revealing the musty interior. A myriad of unhealthy, dark colors greeted Jeremy with open arms. He could almost hear them inviting him to imbibe.

Just close the cupboard and leave!

His fingers released the handle and reached into the cupboard. The tip of his middle finger brushed against the glass of a whiskey bottle. It was cold to the touch, and that only made him realize how parched he was. He licked his lips and gulped. It did nothing to chase away the feeling of sand inside his mouth.

He could imagine uncapping the bottle and drinking. The cold beverage would burn his mouth and throat, but it would be such a beautiful burn. It would be the burn he so desperately craved.

Just one sip. Just one.

But it won't be one, and you know it.

He did. One sip would barely be enough to get a taste of the liquid before it dissolved in his mouth. It would only open his desire to drink more. One sip would turn into "Well, that sip was a small one so it doesn't count." Then that would turn into "One is too close to zero, so might as well take two or three." By the time the third gulp was down his throat, he wouldn't see the point in stopping until the entire bottle was downed.

But the truth of the matter was that he didn't care. He knew well how bad it was for him to drink, but resisting the call of the bottle was like resisting a naked woman with a voluptuous body splayed on the bed in front of him.

He *wanted* to get drunk. He *needed* it. He didn't care about after. He only cared about what he wanted now, now, now.

"How's lunch coming along?" Dannie's voice caused his hand to jerk.

That, in turn, caused the whiskey bottle to clink against the one behind it. A moment of clairvoyance washed over Jeremy. The illusion of the respite the drink promised to provide was gone, popped like an overinflated balloon. He stared at the bottle of whiskey; a snake showing its fangs now that it had been exposed.

He'd almost given in to the urge to drink. What the fuck was he thinking?

Jeremy slammed the cupboard shut and stepped back as if he'd just gotten burned. His fingers closed around the wrist that had reached toward the cupboard. The shaking of his fingers was unbearable. A weakness slithered up his extremities and into his torso, nestling deep inside his gut.

The mac and cheese squelched in the pot. Jeremy ran up to the stove and stirred the pot with a wooden spoon. The meal was pretty much done. He turned off the burner and leaned over the sink, short-breathed. His palms dug into the edge of the sink to hold himself steady. His arms shook like branches in the wind. Ringing filled his ears.

Another panic attack. Great.

If his desire for alcohol had ever been stronger than this, then he didn't remember it. Jeremy's eyes fixated on the glass inside the sink. He'd planned on washing it earlier but never got around to it. He grabbed the glass and raised it under the tap, his hand barely able to hold the weight of it. He ran water into the glass.

At the sight and sound of the water, his mouth went even drier. He brought the glass to his mouth and chugged the water before the glass was half full. The water ran down his chin and fell onto his sweater. When the glass was empty, he drank two more, and then he splashed some water on his face.

The cold liquid felt good, rejuvenating. He could breathe again. His arms and legs stopped quavering. Jeremy swiped his hand under the water running from the tap and swung it to the back of his neck. The cold made his skin prickle with goosebumps, but it was a good feeling. A great feeling.

He didn't move from the sink yet, though. He wanted to be sure that the panic attack was gone. In the past, he'd gotten cocky a few times and thought it was over, but then it came back with a blinding force. Jeremy knew he couldn't beat this thing with brute strength—just like a good swimmer couldn't outswim the waves during a storm. He had to bide his time and wait for it to pass before resuming his regular activities.

It was still there, in the vicinity, waiting for him to let his guard down so it could flank him. Jeremy closed his eyes and took deep breaths just like he was taught.

"I'm eating a burger, by the way," Dannie said. The sentence sounded like she had her mouth full. "How did I get a burger? Well, glad you asked. I actually bought one on the way to work. I was going to save it for dinner, but I figured, screw it, why not eat it while it's still hot? I'll be eating plenty of cold food for the next two months, so I might as well savor this."

Please, stop talking.

Jeremy stared at the dirty dishes in the sink, focusing on his breathing. It wasn't becoming any easier.

"Now, I'm not usually a burger person, but there's this place on the way out of the city called Bentley's BBQ. It's a small place. A dump, really. It's one of those places that would appear on the front pages of the news with a headline like, 'Rat meat found in burgers.'" A short pause ensued. Jeremy imagined Dannie chewing her bite. "Anyway, I've seen Bentley's BBQ on my way to the beach many times, but I never stopped there because, you know. Who would stop at a small burger place in the middle of nowhere when you have so many good hot dog and burger stands at the beach, right?"

More silence. Breathing was slightly easier.

"But then I remembered when I was a kid and my mom used to take me to this one diner off I-295 whenever we visited Grandma. It was called Mike's Bridge Diner. It was one of those places where you'd expect to get the kind of food you'd need to poke with your fork to make sure it was dead. "

A sigh that was supposed to be laughter left Jeremy's mouth. The gesture surprised him.

"And my mom didn't have money back then. My dad was unemployed, and the job market was hard, you know? I remember us sitting at that diner and her going through her wallet, digging out the few remaining five-dollar bills, and I still remember the sour look on her face. I was eight back then, but I knew what that look meant."

Jeremy sucked in a breath of air and nodded. He was well acquainted with financial struggles.

"So, when the waitress arrived and my mom asked me what I wanted to eat, I said I wasn't hungry even though I was starving. My mom said I had to eat, but I just shook my head. Eventually, after not being able to get an answer out of me, she ordered me a burger. The waitress was getting impatient, so I guess she just wanted her to stop breathing down our necks and for me to eat something."

Jeremy felt his strength returning sufficiently enough to straighten his back. He wiped his sleeve across his forehead and grabbed onto the pot full of mac and cheese. Carefully, he transferred a portion that would serve as lunch onto a plate. The cheesy smell that invaded his nostrils made his stomach rumble. The talk of Bentley's burger must have contributed to that, too.

"I asked why she didn't order anything for herself, and she used the same excuse I'd given her. Anyway, it was the best burger I'd had in forever. It was so greasy you could squeeze the oil out of it, and the buns and fries were dry, but it was the best thing ever. But I felt guilty about eating the burger all by myself. So, I slid the remaining half to my mom and told her I was full."

Jeremy let out a hearty chuckle. The sound was foreign to him. Children somehow had good intuition when it came to noticing a change in their parents' behavior.

"She told me to take at least a few more bites, but I grabbed my stomach and faked being full. I could have eaten the whole thing right there, but I wanted my mom to have it. I could tell she was hungry, too. She hadn't eaten anything since the cheese crackers that morning. She ate the other half, and seeing her wolf down that meal felt as good as eating it."

Jeremy lowered the plate on the table and slid into the chair. His legs cried out in relief. He hated admitting it, but Dannie's story interested him.

"We went to Mike's Bridge Diner many more times on our visits to Grandma. That's even where I spent my first paycheck. Can you imagine that? Such a dump being a host to so many fond memories?"

"Those places—those kinds of dumps—they usually are the ones we get the most emotionally attached to," Jeremy said.

He didn't know what compelled him to respond to Dannie. Perhaps he thought that she needed some words of assurance.

"Yeah," Dannie said.

Jeremy stabbed a piece of macaroni onto his fork. It was steaming, so he decided not to stuff it in his mouth just yet, no matter how hungry he was. He glanced at the radio, waiting for Dannie to add something to her story. When that didn't happen, he asked, "Do you still go to Mike's Bridge Diner?"

"No. I stopped going when I was twenty-two."

"Why?"

Jeremy blew on the impaled macaroni and put it into his mouth. The panic attack was all but gone now, but he was still wary.

"Because that's when my mom died."

Shit.

62

Jeremy's jaw worked rapidly to grind the pasta enough for him to swallow it. He held the radio up to his face, his finger lingering gently on the button but not pushing it.

"Sorry," he finally said, because he didn't know what else to say.

"It's okay."

Jeremy was on the verge of asking Dannie how her mom had died, but he didn't want to be rude. It was obviously a painful topic. As if reading his mind, Dannie's response came seconds later.

"Cancer." The clipped word cut through the air. "By the time the doctors found it, it was too late. All I could do was, you know, say my goodbyes."

Jeremy swallowed. The mac and cheese suddenly looked less appealing.

"Anyway, I tried going back to Mike's Diner a couple of times, but it was too painful, you know? I actually went back there some years later, and the place was no longer there. Guess their artery-clogging burgers weren't enough to keep the business running."

Silence draped the air. Jeremy sensed that Dannie had something else to add.

"So, yeah. I guess I thought Bentley's BBQ would bring back some good memories for me."

"And did it?"

"It did. But it was bittersweet. Anyway, yeah. When you go home, stop by over there. He's on Forest Avenue. Get the bacon cheeseburger. It's out of this world."

Dannie's tone closed the topic. Jeremy knew better than to pry with some more questions.

Everyone's running.

He wondered if that was what Dannie was running from. Something told him her mother's death was only a drop in the ocean.

"Well, it'll be at least a month until I can taste a burger," he said as he stabbed another handful of pasta onto the fork.

He tried to remember when the last time he ate a burger was. He couldn't recall. Burgers from a place close to his apartment were his go-to meal whenever his body warned him that he wasn't taking in enough proteins, but after being away from the city for five months, going downstairs and crossing the street to buy fast food felt like a distant memory to him. Besides, it was only food. He ate only because he had to. Because it was what his body required him to do so that he wouldn't fall apart.

I sure could go for a bacon cheeseburger, though, he thought as he stuffed another fork full of cheesy macaroni into his mouth.

CHAPTER 7

Rain pelleted the roof and windows. Thunder exploded somewhere in the distance. Jeremy glanced out the window in the direction of the lighthouse where the dark clouds had flocked, towering above the structure, obscuring the meager rays of the setting sun.

The waves violently crashed against the cliffside, splashing ocean water everywhere. Some of them went as high as the second floor of the lighthouse. Despite the battering of the waves, the lighthouse stood firm, an impregnable bulwark against the relentless onslaught.

"They said this'll be the worst storm in years," Dannie said. "Communication with HQ might get scrambled."

"Not like anything ever happens here anyway."

Jeremy stepped away from the window and plopped onto the couch, the radio still clutched in his hand. With the tasks done for the day, he thought about what to do until bedtime, which would be in a few hours. Back in the city, Jeremy couldn't fall asleep before 4 a.m. The lighthouse seemed to work as a different dimension. Despite having a messed-up sleeping pattern, he was able to fall asleep by midnight on his first night on the job.

"What do you do on nights like these?" Dannie asked.

"I don't know. Nothing, I guess."

"Nothing?"

"Yeah."

Pause.

"Okay, but… you have to do something. Even when you're not doing anything. Like, are you staring at the ceiling, or what?"

More pause. Jeremy sensed confusion on Dannie's end. It amused him.

"I just listen to the rain until I fall asleep." Jeremy shrugged.

A flash illuminated the window for a second. A crack of thunder followed.

"I see," Dannie said.

Jeremy crossed his arms at his chest. He stared at his distorted reflection in the TV. His eyelids were becoming heavy. He allowed them to close. If he fell asleep in the meantime, so be it. He realized that Dannie's voice would probably snap him out of his nap, but he was already well on his way to dreamland that he wouldn't stop and tell her to tone it down.

He stood up and walked into the kitchen. He knew he didn't actually stand up. He was dreaming. He was in the state between being awake and being consumed by deep sleep; an undefined limbo.

Jeremy opened the cupboard with the drinks. He knew he could do so in his dreams without consequences. The liquor bottles awaited him. He grabbed a whiskey bottle by the neck and opened it. Two pills were clutched in his hand. He popped them into his mouth and washed them down with a gulp of the searing drink.

It felt heavenly.

Tap-tap-tap.

It wasn't the rain. Among the battering on the roof, the distinct sound came clearly, perforating the interior.

Tap-tap-tap.

Jeremy turned around. The sound came from the living room. He sauntered back inside and looked around. Nothing was in sight. Lightning exploded in the distance.

Tap-tap-tap.

The sound was glassy like tea cups being set back on their plates. Jeremy's eyes sprang to the window.

Tap-tap-tap.

A finger jabbed the pane of glass. Lightning exploded in the distance, a flash bathing the exterior in light. A finger pressed against the window came into view. The hand was closed in a fist, the pointer bent into a hook, tapping against the glass.

Tap-tap-tap.

Jeremy opened his eyes and blinked the blur away. He turned his head to the window.

Nothing but the droplets of rain trickling down the glass.

He swallowed. He swore that he could taste whiskey on his tongue from the vivid dream. He stood up and sauntered to the window, peeking outside. It was getting dark fast. The rain showered the outside in heavy quantities. Jeremy craned his neck to look as far left and right as he could. His eyes then fell on the window itself. He squinted at the tiny stain that the bullets of rain were washing away. At the—

A loud staticky sound exploded in the room.

Jeremy jerked around, his heart plummeting into his gut.

"Called it. Comms with HQ aren't working," Dannie said.

Jeremy's shoulders drooped. "Jesus *fucking* Christ."

It felt good to say that aloud. No cussing felt as good as religious cussing. It was like Jeremy's defiance to the god he hated so much.

He sat back on the couch, ignoring the radio. It couldn't have been more than a few minutes since he'd closed his eyes, and yet, it felt like hours had gone by. He was irritable, just like he was after every nap he took. More than that, a hankering harpooned him.

Back when he was younger, his body demanded something packed with sugar whenever he woke up from his midday nap. Later on, that sugar craving was replaced by a darker desire. Something that had horrible taste but muted all his issues after just a few sips.

Jeremy had always liked imbibing here and there but in permissible quantities. At every family reunion on Nadine's side, drinking was the only thing that helped him stay sane until the get-together was over. He had dealt with all sorts of crazy, demanding, and unreasonable clients during his career, but his wife's family was a whole different story.

The constant yelling, the mandatory annual arguments between Nadine's grandpa and uncle that often ended up with one of them storming out, the racist and sexual jokes—all of it was excuse enough for Jeremy to drink during reunions.

Nadine's prying family didn't really like that. On one occasion, her grandpa pulled Jeremy aside to talk to him. He hugged him and told him everything would be okay and that he was here for him if he needed help with his struggles.

He got teary-eyed when he spoke about his father, who had been consumed by alcoholism and had lost his job and family. Jeremy had found the situation too amusing to try to justify himself. Instead, he smiled, nodded, and thanked Nadine's grandpa for his support during such a "difficult time."

Slowly, the drinking did become heavier, even if it happened only at the reunions. But then the call that changed Jeremy's life catapulted him into binge drinking. And this time, there was nothing amusing about it.

"How's it looking over there, Jer?" Dannie asked.

Jeremy's cheek twitched at the nickname. He grimaced at the radio before taking it into his hand. "What do you think?"

"Thinking of going on a little surf?"

"No. I'm a terrible surfer."

68

"Still. It must be nice waking up next to the beach every day."

"Not for me. I hate beaches."

"What? Really? Are you sure you picked the right job?"

"I'm a lighthouse keeper, not a lifeguard."

Thunder ripped outside, a sudden crack that caused Jeremy to jerk his head to the window.

"What… possibly… th… ach?" Dannie's voice came as chopped out.

"Repeat that last. You cut off," Jeremy said.

Silence.

"Dannie. Can you hear me?"

It was the first time he'd said her name. It felt strange, awkward. It felt too *personal*, and he hated it.

Khhh.

"The weather must be messing with our radios, huh?" This time, her voice came through clearly.

"Yeah."

"Hey, are we sure using them now is safe? Like, what if the devices, like, lure in thunder? We could get killed."

A lopsided smile curved the corner of Jeremy's lip. He was tempted to tell her as a joke that it was, indeed, dangerous to use radios now and that she should put it as far away as possible and not speak. It occurred to him that he had spent almost the entire day talking to Dannie on the radio. It was so out of his character.

At the same time, he had to admit that talking to her was not as annoying as he initially thought it'd be. He enjoyed the solitude in the lighthouse, but he hadn't realized until today how much he missed talking, like, really *talking*, to someone.

Earlier, when he'd had a panic attack, Dannie's voice soothed him. The story about her mom and Mike's Bridge Diner were enough to take Jeremy's mind off things, and that, in turn, helped calm him down. She'd helped him even though she wasn't aware of it.

He wanted to thank her for it, but that would require explaining his state, which would, in turn, open up the floodgates that he'd worked so hard on keeping closed. Plus, his pride wouldn't allow him to do so. He liked being clammed up. It was safer that way. Predictable.

"Yeah, it's safe," he finally said.

"Okay, cool. For a moment there, I thought I'd have to spend the whole night in silence."

"Right. You said something before when you cut off."

"Oh, right. I was asking what you didn't like about beaches. I mean, the weather's always nice and warm, there's sand, and the water's right there to cool you off if you get too hot. Nothing quite as pleasant as gentle waves crashing into you while you're standing waist-deep in water, with your feet gliding and sinking into the soft sand."

"It's always too hot for my taste. I can't stand in the sun for too long. Sand is annoying. It makes it hard to walk. Okay for the water, but five minutes in, and I've already had enough."

"So, do you ever jump into the water over there? I mean, you're practically paid to be on the beach for six months. Any other normal human being would kill for such a job."

"Not me. White Mars sounds more appealing."

Tinny laughter came from the radio. Dannie's laugh was genuine, and that's what made it so pretty. Jeremy stood up and returned to the window. The sky had gone from hues of dark gray to abyssal black. The lantern of the lighthouse had started working, its cone rotating in a steady circle, sweeping the sky.

"Besides, this isn't a good place for a vacation. Even for a beach fan," Jeremy said.

"Why not?"

"It's all sharp rocks and tall cliffs. You wouldn't be able to sunbathe unless you're looking for acupuncture at the same time. And the water's always too cold."

"Ouch. Way to break my illusion, Grinch."

"I'm just telling you how it is."

"I think it still beats being stuck in a tower surrounded by tall trees. Seriously, I can't see anything from the white pines here."

Jeremy visualized Dannie's workplace for a moment. A rectangular room with windows on all sides, looking out into the trees and the night sky. A control panel with comms devices would occupy one side of the room. A bed, a nightstand, and perhaps a TV would sit in one corner. There would probably be a desk and a tiny kitchenette there, too, and perhaps a heater for the cold nights.

Since the control tower had to be high up, Dannie would need to go down the stairs to reach the ground, and then? Maybe a single trail that would lead back to the city but too far for walking.

"Well, I have to disagree," Jeremy said. "I'd take the woods over the beach any—"

The words died in his throat when the lantern on the lighthouse went out.

Jeremy squinted at the dimly visible white and red stripes of the lighthouse, his nose pressed against the cold glass.

"Jeremy? Did we cut off again?"

"Hold on a minute," Jeremy said absent-mindedly.

He continued staring at the lighthouse, waiting for the lantern to come back on. Maybe the storm somehow messed with it, but it would come back on soon. That's what he hoped for, but the longer he stared, the more he came to terms with the fact that he would need to go out in the rain to fix it.

However, before he did that, he would first make sure that everything was okay with the automation panel. It was very possible that the lightning had somehow damaged the electronics, and if that were the case, then fixing it would most likely be beyond Jeremy's skills.

He opened the door to the service room and flipped on the light switch. The bevy of lights on the panel blinked and glowed. Jeremy picked up the manual from the workbench and leafed through the pages, looking for a section in the book that would match the problem he was having.

Once he located the "HOW TO CHECK IF EVERYTHING IS IN WORKING ORDER" chapter, he flipped to that page and rapidly traced his finger along the text. There were only a couple of steps to make sure everything was okay.

"Green light for rotation, okay. It's green." He looked up from the manual to the panel and then back to the book. "Light for manual lantern should be off. Okay. The one next to it is supposed to blink. Okay, it's blinking."

One by one, Jeremy went through each step. The closer he got to the end, the more desperate he became because, if everything was in working order, he wouldn't know what to do.

"During storms, it's possible that a fuse might get fried," he read. "Okay, here we go. Let's see… Open the panel as indicated in the picture below and pull out the fuse."

Jeremy did as instructed on the page. He knelt down, unlocked the panel at the bottom, and opened it. After inspecting the fuse and comparing it to the one in the picture, he deduced that the fuse was not the problem. Only one step remained.

"If you have completed all the above steps and the lighthouse is still not functional, go to the lantern room and check if everything is okay with the lantern. Instructions on how to check the lantern are on page 59. Great."

Jeremy closed the panel, stood up, and stared at the buttons. He went through all the steps once more just to make sure he didn't miss anything. When everything was in order the second time around, he gave it a third go.

Then he finally became convinced that there was no other choice than to go out to the lighthouse. Cursing under his breath, he walked out to the foyer and donned the raincoat that hung on the wall.

"Jeremy? Everything okay over there?" The radio crackled.

"The lighthouse just went out. I have to see what's wrong."

"Wait, you have to go outside and check it? In this weather?"

"Yeah." Jeremy flung the hoodie over his head and pulled out the dirty rubber boots from the shoe stand.

The last time he wore them was in late December. He'd thrown them into the shoe stand after using them, dirty as they were, and he hadn't looked at them since. He'd forgotten how tight and uncomfortable they were until his foot slid inside. He wiggled his toes and heel to make some room.

"That sounds dangerous. Maybe you should wait for the storm to calm down," Dannie said.

"Can't."

"Why not?"

"Because if there are any ships out there in this storm, they'll want to know where they are. And if they're close, they could crash if they don't see the light."

"Does the lighthouse shine so far?"

"Around twenty nautical miles."

Silence.

"It's about twenty-three miles."

"Okay, that's brighter than I thought."

"Yeah."

Jeremy stuffed the manual into the pocket of his pants, hoping it wouldn't get soaked in the rain. His hopes for that diminished when he opened the door and looked at the torrential rain outside. The staticky noise was deafening. The droplets found their way across the threshold and were already licking Jeremy's boots and shins even with the roof awning that protruded.

He would be soaked the moment he stepped outside.

"Okay, listen. I'm going out now," he said. "I'll leave the radio here because I don't want it to get wet."

"Just hurry back, all right?"

"Yeah."

Jeremy placed the radio on the shoe stand, cinched his hoodie, and stepped out into the rain.

CHAPTER 8

The moment he had no roof for protection above his head was the moment the external noises grew in intensity. The only sounds that existed were the pellets of rain pattering all around him and all over him, a *tap-tap-tap-tap* similar to an automatic rifle hitting his protective hoodie. Even his own panting was inaudible, despite the hoodie that draped his head.

Jeremy raced across the slippery ground, his boots splashing the deep puddles of water. The droplets had already perforated his pants, the cold liquid pressed tightly against the skin of his thighs. His hands were drenched as if he had dipped them into a bucket of cold water. His fingers had gone numb.

Jeremy held his head down, but that did nothing to stop the rain from blowing into his face. The wind was relentless. Jeremy plodded across the slick rocks, careful how he stepped on them. The waves crashed all around him, reaching record heights and draping the pathway in foam and water.

Getting wet was inevitable.

Whenever Jeremy found himself in rainy weather like this one, he remembered the experiment he'd seen years ago on TV. It was about a theory that suggested that running through the rain would cause the person to become wetter than it would if they walked through the rain.

Although he never understood the reasoning behind it, he tested it out multiple times, but he never saw any visible results. With rain as relentless as the one tonight, he was sure that it didn't matter whether someone walked, ran, crawled, or flew from point A to point B.

They would be just as drenched the moment they poked their heads out.

A swell of water crashed into Jeremy's left, shooting icy daggers through his legs and making him wobbly where he stood. Jeremy tottered to the side and put his hands out in front of himself to stop the fall. His palms skidded across the slippery ground. He fell flat on his chest, his face missing a sharp rock by mere inches.

Son of a bitch!

His abraded palms burned. Before he could get himself up, another wave slammed on top of him. The water that crashed on his head felt like a whack from a baseball bat. For a second, a watery roar filled his ears as the wave submerged him, his nostrils snorting the salty water.

Jeremy coughed just as the splash receded, his nose and eyes burning.

Fucking shit!

Jeremy clambered to his feet and trudged toward the lighthouse, which was so close now. Another wave washed his back, but this one was barely a mosquito sting compared to the crash before. Jeremy broke into a clumsy dash across the remainder of the path and burst through the door of the lighthouse.

***

"Fucking rain." He threw the hoodie back and ran his fingers through his wet hair and down his face.

He took a moment to catch his breath. He upturned his palms to see the damage. The skin had been scratched a little, but nothing serious. The burn was annoying, though. Jeremy wiped his palms on the raincoat and looked at the stairs awaiting his climb.

Drenched, he felt twenty pounds heavier. Water had entered his boots and soaked his socks, creating a squelching sound with each step he took. The waves that ran outside raged. He thought he could hear the water splashing just on the other side of the wall, the thin barrier the only protection from being swallowed by the unforgiving ocean.

He needed a moment by the time he reached the bedroom, and then another when he climbed into the living room. Lightning flashed outside, revealing the "14 DEAD IN SCHOOL SHOOTING, SUSPECT SHOT BY POLICE" paper standing at the edge of the kitchen table, turned upside down, glaring at Jeremy.

He shook his head and stalked out of the room. The control room was quieter than the lower floors. Although the pattering of the rain and the smiting of thunder were still potent, the lapping of the waves had quieted down, now merely a soft summer breeze.

Jeremy walked across the room in the dark and opened the drawers, his fingers blindly feeling for the flashlight. When his hand closed around the familiar tubular object, he grasped it with both hands and traced a finger to the bottom to find the button. When he flicked it on to see if it worked, the bright beam of blueish light speared the air.

He swept the flashlight around and then fixed the cone on the stairs leading up. By the time he reached the lantern room, his quadriceps were burning from exertion. The wet clothes that clung to his skin were irritating. He thought about changing out of his clothes, bundling himself into a bunch of blankets, and unwinding with—

No. Don't even go there.

The lantern room was still and dark. He'd never been up there at night, so under the scintillating beam of the flashlight, the room looked foreign. Before he could begin his work, he reached into his pocket and searched for the manual.

One touch was enough to tell him how utterly soaked it was. Jeremy let out a sigh as he fished the book out and illuminated it under the flashlight. The pages were wavy and wrinkled, the ink smudged, droplets of seawater dribbling off of it.

Jeremy squeezed the flashlight between his cheek and shoulder and leafed through the first page. It was too loose, as if just waiting to fall apart. When he pinched the corner of the next page and pulled, it ripped.

No good.

Jeremy gently placed the book on the floor to let it dry. In the meantime, he decided to still take a look at the lantern and see if he could figure out what was wrong.

Step by step, he circled the lantern, shining the flashlight on every inch of the lighthouse's most important asset, trying to find something faulty. A full circle later, Jeremy was scratching the top of his head. Lightning exploded in the distance. Jeremy caught the moment it struck in the sky like a crack on the floor imbued with incandescence.

The roiling waves far under the lighthouse made Jeremy dizzy. It almost made it look like the lighthouse was riding the waves, climbing and descending the gradients created by the water's surface. He averted his gaze from the sight and returned to the manual soaking the floor.

Crouching down, he carefully thumbed through the edge of the pages until he had a hold of the first one. Flipping it prudently, he illuminated the table of contents and located the chapter called "INSTRUCTIONS ON HOW TO CHECK THE LANTERN." Page 59.

The ink on page 59 was badly smudged, giving the letters the appearance of reading without glasses. Jeremy's finger traced the lines of text, his lips soundlessly moving as he read the instructions. He lingered on one particular sentence that caught his attention. "The button to turn the lantern on and off manually is located under—as shown in the picture."

He whispered that sentence three more times, then looked at the picture, comparing it to the real thing. He stood up, walking around the rim of the lantern, his flashlight illuminating the thin, circular ridge. Halfway through, he saw it.

A small bump outside the ridge that he immediately recognized as a button. Jeremy knelt and brought the flashlight closer. He expected to see a button, but it was actually an on/off switch. OFF was pressed down, mocking Jeremy.

He shook his head at the absurdity of the lighthouse's design. His hand reached forward, hovering above ON, but he hesitated. He thought about what would happen if he was wrong.

There's nothing you can do to mess up the lighthouse, so don't be afraid to play around with the buttons and switches, Matthew had told him just before he had left.

With that encouragement, Jeremy shrugged and pressed down on the button.

***

The light that came to life before Jeremy hurt his eyes. He fell backward in surprise, raising a hand in front of him to shield his face from the brightness, his eyes squeezed shut. He'd never stood a foot away from a functioning lighthouse lantern at night and didn't know if it was powerful enough to blind a person at that range.

"Fucking hell!" he muttered just as a loud whirring filled the room.

The light was out of his face. Jeremy opened his eyes, his vision obscured by the floaters induced by the bright light. They looked like splotches of paint on a canvas.

Before he could react properly, the lantern had rotated full circle and swept above Jeremy once more.

The whirring grew louder and louder like a car's engine trying to pull out max speed. It made Jeremy uneasy. It gave him the impression that the lantern would explode when the whirring reached a certain level.

Not waiting to see what would happen, Jeremy crawled on his hands and knees toward the exit. The whirring became muffled the moment he slammed the lantern room shut behind him. He slid his palm across the wall as he made his way down the stairs, the floaters in his vision slowly fading. He blinked hard in hopes of chasing them away, but they refused to leave. He looked toward the corners of his eyeballs, but the floaters annoyingly followed him wherever his pupils went.

By the time he made it back downstairs, his vision was clear, but then another problem awaited him: running back to the house. He stared through the open door at the narrow pathway and the house that offered sanctuary.

Dry clothes awaited him there. He could brew some hot tea. He was hungry, too. He still had mac and cheese from lunch.

He licked his lips, leaving a salty taste lingering on his tongue. A tall wave loudly crashed into the pathway, as if to disperse Jeremy's hopes of making it back without trouble. Jeremy sighed, pulled the hoodie over his head, and braced himself for another volley. He tucked the flashlight under his raincoat, hoping to keep it safe until he was back under the roof.

He jackknifed, like a sprinter getting ready to race, and propelled himself from his heel forward, into the belly of the beast.

***

"Goddammit," he said when he reached the roof awning.

He was out of breath. His lungs burned. Most of all, he was wet, and it annoyed the hell out of him. Jeremy opened the door and stumbled inside before slamming it shut, significantly decreasing the volume of the outside noise.

He slithered out of the raincoat and let it plop to the ground, not giving a shit. He kicked the rubber boots off. Water slid off of them and poured out of them. A large puddle covered the foyer. Jeremy took his clothes off and threw them on the floor where the raincoat was. His skin was cold to the touch, and he was starting to sniffle.

"Jeremy? Hello?" the radio next to him spoke, giving him a momentary fright. "Can you repeat what you just said?"

When Jeremy was in his underwear, he picked up the radio and walked into the bedroom. "Um, I didn't say anything."

"No, I heard you pushing the button to talk, but no voice came through."

"You must have heard wrong. I just stepped inside the house a second ago."

"No, the radio definitely buzzed."

Jeremy opened the drawers and pulled out a fresh pair of pants, a t-shirt, underwear, socks, and a towel.

"Might be because of the storm." Jeremy threw the radio on the bed and took off his underwear.

"I guess you're right. Was everything okay at the lighthouse?"

Jeremy wiped his hair with the towel, hung it around his neck, and picked up the radio to respond. "Yeah. The manual switch was on. Must have been something the weather caused."

"How bad is it out there?"

"Pretty fucking bad. I almost broke my neck on my way there."

"What? Really? Are you okay?"

"Yeah. Just drenched. Had to change out of my clothes. I hope the lighthouse doesn't malfunction again tonight."

He dried off his body and put on the clean set of clothes. He already felt much better without the weight of the soggy fabric clinging to his skin. He felt like he still needed food.

And a drink. Not an alcoholic one but something warm to get rid of the iciness that had nestled in his body. More than anything, he needed rest. Today was pretty exhausting, and he felt that he'd earned a long break. Jeremy walked out into the living room and approached the window.

"Hey, I just got a message from HQ," Dannie said. "It says they sent this two hours ago, but it just now got through."

"What does it say?"

"Lock the doors and stay inside."

"Cryptic."

"I guess they expect this storm to last for a while, huh?"

"Maybe."

Some silence lingered in the air.

"Hey, you're not going to bed yet, are you?" Dannie asked.

"Maybe. Why?"

"Because I'm not sleepy yet, and I'll get bored if you leave."

Jeremy didn't feel sleepy, either. His body was heavy with exhaustion, but it was one of those feelings of tiredness where he would be too sluggish to do something productive and too active to fall asleep. He hated that feeling.

"I guess I won't be going to bed yet," he said.

"Nice!" Excitement coated Dannie's voice. "We can play some games. How about trivia?"

Jeremy nodded, but he wasn't listening. Nodding his head was a muscle memory that he'd carried from his old job. Even when he was on a call with a client, he would nod until he remembered that the client couldn't see his face.

"Uh, yeah. Sure," he said belatedly.

His eyes were fixed on the rotating beam on top of the lighthouse's dome.

CHAPTER 9

It was almost 11 p.m. Jeremy glanced at the lighthouse every couple of minutes, even though he didn't know what he was doing that for. For some reason, he couldn't shake the feeling of anticipation. Perhaps he was waiting for the lighthouse to malfunction again?

He told himself that if he didn't know the lighthouse wasn't working, he wouldn't need to fix it, but still, something wouldn't let him just ignore it. Maybe it was his sense of duty as a lighthouse keeper. Maybe it was just anxiety over the lightning cracking in the distance that threatened with each boom to cause damage.

Earlier, Jeremy and Dannie had played some trivia games. Jeremy was winning, but it was a close call. Then they stopped keeping track of the score.

After that, they shared scary stories they knew—specifically stories about haunted lighthouses, ghost ships, cursed pirates, and so on. Jeremy had told her about the rumor of the lighthouse he worked at being haunted by the ghost of a keeper who died there. After that, they stopped sharing scary stories.

It all brought Jeremy back to his days of camping with Ray. Ray was only seven back then and really excited to go on the father-son trip to the woods. They sat around the campfire, roasting marshmallows, and Jeremy told stories. Raymond wasn't a fan of ghost stories, so Jeremy instead told him made-up fantasy stories that he knew he'd like: knights slaying dragons to save princesses, poor peasants proving their strength by defeating monsters that no soldier could in decades, forces of good battling against the armies of evil and coming out triumphant.

Ever since seeing *The Lord Of The Rings* in the movie theater, Ray had become obsessed with epic fantasy. He had spent hours drawing the fellowship of the ring, making maps, writing his own stories... He was kind of a nerd, which Jeremy found cute. Unfortunately, that's why Ray got bullied in middle school a lot until Jeremy and Nadine intervened.

The problems stopped for a while after that.

"I could really use some fresh air, but I can't even crank a window over here," Dannie said.

"So open the door," Jeremy croaked.

Even though Jeremy and Dannie weren't in the same room, at moments, it felt like they were. He could almost imagine, based on the color of her voice, how she looked and what her age was. He guessed she was around Jeremy's age, but he didn't want to ask since, in his experience, women winced so much at that question.

The living room was quiet. Dannie's energetic speaking had toned down, which told Jeremy that she was probably going through the same stuff as him—feeling sleepy.

Jeremy sat on the couch, his head hanging backward, his eyelids heavy. He had given in a few times in the past hour and allowed his eyes to close, but he still couldn't fall asleep. Either that or Dannie would startle him with an unrelated question.

"You got a family back home?" her voice pierced the air.

Jeremy raised the radio, pressed the PTT button, then released it. He let out a sigh then pressed the button again. "I have parents in Upstate New York."

But Dannie wasn't asking that, and he knew it.

"I mean, a wife or children. Anything like that?" she asked.

"An ex-wife," he blurted.

Pause on Dannie's end. Perhaps she'd realized that the topic was sensitive.

"How long were you guys married?" she asked.

"Sixteen years."

And four months, Jeremy refrained from adding because he didn't want Dannie to know he paid attention to such details. He didn't want her to know he still lingered on his former marriage and the broken future that could have been.

"*Sixteen* years? Wow. Why separate after such a long time?"

Jeremy could tell her all the details. He could talk for hours about how he and Nadine had drifted apart; how they never talked unless it was to give a cold greeting or goodbye; how when they looked into each other's eyes they saw strangers and not the spouses they'd built their lives with.

It wasn't just the unfamiliarity that had formed between them. There was a profound animosity that Jeremy couldn't shake. Whenever he looked at Nadine, uncontrolled anger took him over. He had to clench his jaw to stop himself from raising his voice at her or smashing something in the house.

She was the same. He could see it in her eyes—that look that hadn't been there in the past sixteen years. When she didn't pity him, she blamed him. She *hated* him. She didn't need to say anything for him to know it. Jeremy stayed later and later in the office, just to avoid that gaze. When he did return home, he'd find the house quiet, Nadine sleeping upstairs, and he would quietly slither onto the living room couch where he would pass out from worry and exhaustion.

Then one morning, Nadine was no longer in the house, her things gone, leaving only the empty drawers and wardrobes. Did it come as a surprise to Jeremy? Absolutely not. He'd expected it for months, so when it finally happened, it was almost a relief.

"It's a complicated story." Jeremy didn't mean for the words to sound so clipped and hostile, but he couldn't help it. The same anger that he felt toward Nadine now surfaced again. Who the hell was this person on the radio to ask him questions about his private life? And to do it so matter-of-factly as if she was asking him about his favorite food.

"Sorry. I didn't mean to pry," Dannie said.

Jeremy's anger deflated as quickly as it had appeared. He closed his eyes and shook his head, silently chiding himself for getting irked. Dannie didn't know.

"And you?" he asked, mostly because he just wanted to chase away the dark thoughts that poked their many tentacles through the bars, reaching for Jeremy's brain like it was a meal.

"No," she said. "I used to be engaged, but never married."

"What happened?"

He realized the irony of him asking the same question that would have angered him, but the dark tentacles were creeping closer, and he desperately needed something to take his mind off things.

"David and I met at work. He was a doctor who worked at the hospital. He and I used to talk during those slow nights. One thing led to another, and we started dating. You know how when you meet someone, you just click right away, and you're just talking over each other because you share so much in common?"

Jeremy knew. That was exactly what it was like for him and Nadine when they met in college.

"David and I dated for a year before he proposed. We moved in together, and that's where things pretty much stopped."

"What do you mean?"

"We both agreed that there was no need to rush with marriage. We were still young, and we just wanted to take it slow and enjoy, you know? So, we never really agreed on a wedding date. As time went on, whenever I asked David about it, he always found an excuse why it wasn't a good time. Then we talked about having a child. For a while, it all revolved around "I'm not ready yet" to "I might be ready someday." But then we *were* ready, and we couldn't do it."

Jeremy listened intently. He already knew that the outcome of Dannie's story would be a sad one, but he was interested in knowing what led to such an ending.

Dannie's speaking speed had become significantly slower at that point. She might have been looking for the right words, or maybe it was difficult to talk about it. Either way, Jeremy didn't interrupt her. "We went to various doctors to see what was wrong. We had all sorts of, um, tests done. David's results came out okay. Mine... mine didn't."

A long silence ensued. Jeremy felt like he should say something. Even something as simple as "sorry," but whenever he opened his mouth, he closed it instead. There was nothing he could say that Dannie hadn't probably already heard a million times over from friends and family.

"After that, things started to change. And the change in him was just so sudden, you know? It's like, the person who I could confide in, the person who would always be there for me, no matter what, was suddenly gone. In a day."

Jeremy knew exactly what she was talking about. The same thing happened to him and Nadine.

"David and I had talked, and we agreed that we didn't need kids. I had tried convincing him to try other methods. Adoption, surrogates, anything else, but he dismissed it. Said everything was okay. And still, I couldn't help but notice how he started resenting me ever since we got the test results."

"He had grown more and more distant. I had known something was wrong. It's not hard to figure these things out when the person in question lives with you. When they go from showering you with attention to barely giving you a peck on the cheek on the way to work, wearing the perfume you hate, and constantly looking distant, you pretty much know what's going on. But the problem is we never want to admit it. I think it's a defense mechanism of the brain, to hold so firmly onto the belief that the person we cherish so much would never do something to hurt us."

Even when the evidence is in plain sight in front of us. Jeremy grinned.

"Hindsight is twenty-twenty, right? Anyway, you can probably guess the rest of this story," Dannie said.

"Maybe." Jeremy frowned.

He had a few guesses, but the one that he assumed fit Dannie's story was the one where she walked in on David in bed with another woman.

"One night, we sat down and talked about everything. It was a friendly conversation. It's one of those conversations where both sides know what's going on, and they just want to find a consensus, you know? We talked. He told me everything. Told me how he was seeing the new doctor behind my back. I demanded to know everything. To this day, I sometimes wish I never asked."

"It hurt like hell to hear him talking about someone the way he should have talked about me. My whole life— everything I'd invested myself into—was falling apart right before my eyes, and there was nothing I could do. And I still remember, even as I listened to him talking about this woman with such fascination and affection, my mind was looking for a solution to fix it all, to take it all back and make things the way they were before."

It was like Jeremy was looking at the reflection of his own, unspoken thoughts.

"But there was no way to fix it," Dannie said, a sense of finality in her tone. "David had pretty much already started his new life with Doctor Sanderson. All I could do, really, was let him go, no matter how much I wanted to fight to get him back. And so, I did that. I still remember, to this day, when I said goodbye that night, he turned around to leave. I kept staring at him as he walked away. He didn't even turn around. And all I could think was, "I'm no longer number one in his life."

Jeremy thought he detected Dannie's voice becoming shaky toward the end.

"I slept in a motel for the next few days until my transfer got approved, and I never saw David again."

"Is that why you quit the job?"

"No. I quit years later when I got sick of seeing all the gore."

"You ever miss it?"

"Some parts of it. But I don't think I'd go back to that job."

"Why not?"

"Too many bad memories."

The pattering of the rain punctuated the air.

"I'm sorry that happened to you," was all Jeremy said.

"Me too."

"When did it all happen?"

"Years ago. But it sometimes feels like yesterday."

"Have you tried dating after David?"

"I have, but I could never commit myself to it properly. It felt like rebuilding my entire life from scratch. It was easier to just ignore it. So I just sort of... gave up on it. What about you?"

"No." Jeremy scoffed. "I guess it's still too fresh in my mind."

"It always feels like that, doesn't it?"

Jeremy leaned back, let out something between a sigh and a peal of laughter, and said, "I guess you were right."

"About what?" Dannie asked.

Her voice sounded lethargic, and Jeremy couldn't tell if it was from the sadness or from being tired. It easily could have been both.

He pushed the PTT button, and after a long delay said, "We're all running from something."

CHAPTER 10

Jeremy closed his eyes and relaxed his body as best he could. One thing he realized helped him fall asleep faster was actually holding his eyes closed. That was easier said than done because the thoughts that often invaded his mind in the unholy hours of the night made it effortless to keep his eyes open and stare at the ceiling.

Doctor Martelle had prescribed Xanax to him to help with his insomnia, and the meds helped for a while, but then they stopped functioning. Jeremy needed to up the dosage to sleep better. After a while, he dropped the medication completely and turned to intense drinking.

It helped, but it came at a heavy cost.

Jeremy's body was weightless, a sure sign that he was drifting into sleep. The pitter-patter of the rain somehow became amplified until it was the only sound Jeremy was aware of.

A loud slam caused him to jerk in his seat.

The sound was accompanied by the louder shower of the rain and the howling of the wind. It was coming from the foyer. Jeremy shot up to his feet and strode to the source of the sound. The front door was wide open, slammed against the wall, allowing intrusive droplets of rain to be carried over the threshold by the strong wind.

"Jesus!" Jeremy ran up to the door and shut it hard.

He locked it this time, annoyed that the wind kept opening it. A cold and wet feeling invaded the bottom of his sock. He looked down at the muddy footprints that he'd left earlier when he returned from the lighthouse.

"Goddammit," he said as he raised his foot to assess the damage.

It was a white sock, and the brown that now stained it was impossible to miss. Jeremy looked at the mud-covered floor. His eyes fell on the rubber boots in front of the shoe stand. One of them was overturned, the sole facing Jeremy. It was wet, but not muddy.

Not muddy.

Jeremy stared down at the tracks of mud in the foyer. On a whim, he unlocked the door and opened it. The microscopic droplets of rain cooled his face. He scanned the area as much as the safety and dryness of the house allowed him to.

A flash of lightning illuminated the desolate area, revealing a soaked, barren land.

Jeremy took a step back and slowly closed the door, turning the lock once more. He turned on the balls of his feet and strode into the living room. As if sensing his arrival, the radio crackled to life. "You're awfully quiet, Jeremy. Did you fall asleep?"

Jeremy snatched the radio off the bed and walked up to the window. "I think there's someone here."

Dannie didn't respond. He could imagine a sheepish stare on her face as she processed what he said.

"What?" she asked.

"I think there's someone outside the house." Jeremy's eyes darted across the empty area outside for any movement. Aside from the rotating lantern of the lighthouse and the particles of rain that showered, nothing was out there.

"That's impossible. Why would anyone be there at this time? And in this storm?" Dannie asked.

Thunder whacked just above the house, loud enough to shake the windows in their frames. Jeremy fervently scrutinized the area outside under the split-second-long illumination of the lightning. Nothing.

"Jeremy?" Dannie sounded timid, like approaching a dangerous wild animal.

"I'm going outside to check it out," Jeremy said.

"What? Are you sure that's a good idea? What if it's dangerous?"

Jeremy was already in the foyer, donning the raincoat. It was still soggy on the inside. "If someone's out there, they might need help."

"But what if *(khhh)*… not what y *(khhh)*…ang *(khh)*."

"Dannie, you're breaking up. Listen, I'll be back in a minute. Just going to take a look outside."

Jeremy slid into the wet rubber boots. The sensation of the cold water penetrating through his socks and sticking to the skin of his feet was annoying. He ignored it as he pulled the hoodie over his head and unlocked the door. He put the radio on the shoe stand, grabbed the flashlight, and stepped outside once more into the cold rain.

***

He didn't want to risk going too far out from the safety of the house before making sure it was okay to do so. Jeremy's will for self-preservation may have been low, but he wasn't stupid enough to walk out there without looking for some maniac to whack him over the head.

The cone of the flashlight that swept the area illuminated nothing but the falling droplets. Jeremy closed the door behind him, his body tense, his senses all on edge.

He stepped forward, the awning of the roof no longer shielding him from the unrelenting rain. He pivoted left and right, slowly illuminating every crag and rock that might have resembled a person.

"Hello?" he called out, his voice muffled by the shower. "Hello?!" he shouted again, his voice cracking this time, but at least it was louder.

No response, other than the gust of wind that whipped his face. Jeremy turned and walked alongside the house. He

96

didn't stay close to the walls so that he would have enough time to react in case someone jumped him from the corner. The beam of the flashlight controlled by his hand became jittery every time he illuminated the corner of the house, fully expecting a ragged, dirty man with an unkempt beard and long hair to come into view.

He also kept an eye out on the surrounding area. For the first time since he started working at the lighthouse, he was grateful that flatlands surrounded him, and not a terrain that would allow whoever was close by to get the jump on him.

When he finished walking a full circle around the house and was back at the front door, the tension that had firmly held his gut eased its grip a little. Jeremy swiveled the flashlight across the area once more, satisfied that no one was there.

His shoulders drooped. He threw his head back to ease up the tension in his neck and closed his eyes. The rain that cooled his face felt good. He opened his eyes, ready to go inside.

And then his eyes fell on the silhouette standing against the lantern on top of the lighthouse.

CHAPTER 11

There he was.

Standing on the walkway of the dome, superimposed against the lantern, staring down at Jeremy as if mocking him.

It wasn't someone in need of help. If it was, then they would have gone to the house instead. No, this was something different. This was some asshole trying to be funny.

Seeing him at the top of the lighthouse provoked no fear in Jeremy. Instead, rage crashed over him, powerful like the waves that sloshed around the pathway. Jeremy's lips retracted into his mouth from the hard scrunching, and before he knew it, he was striding toward the lighthouse.

The water that splashed his sides was nothing. He was a truck barreling through all obstacles, unstoppable by mother nature. As much as he wanted to fix his eyes on the figure above, the craggy ground made it impossible, no matter how much fury fueled him.

His eyes were trained on the lighthouse door. He couldn't reach it fast enough. When he did, he shoved the door open so hard it slammed against the wall. He wanted the stalker to know he was coming. He wanted him to know he was messing with the wrong person.

He closed the door behind him and locked it. The intruder was not going anywhere.

Jeremy raced upstairs, his flashlight pointed at the top, his heart pummeling his chest uncontrollably. He didn't stop when he reached the living quarters. He gave the room one aloof sweep of the light to make sure it was empty and then continued plodding upstairs.

The bedroom was empty as well.

And so was the communications room.

The higher Jeremy climbed, the more nervous he became. In the comms room, Jeremy scooped up a metal pipe from under the desk. It had been there ever since he'd arrived, and although he didn't know what part the pipe used to belong to, Jeremy never touched it because he didn't know how important it was.

Now, it was like this was its purpose the entire time— to serve as a weapon for Jeremy to defend himself and stave off the intruder.

The pipe felt heavy in his hand. Swinging it would be slow, but he hoped that he wouldn't need to swing it. Just the appearance of it should have been enough to frighten the intruder into surrendering.

Unless he's armed with something deadlier, the thought wormed into Jeremy's mind for the first time since he entered the lighthouse.

He didn't want to entertain it. If he did, then fear might get the better of him, and he might end up running back to the house and locking himself in the bathroom until morning. It was the intruder who should be afraid, not him.

Jeremy tensed up his shoulders when he approached the stairs. He pointed the flashlight up. The stairs swerved toward the lantern room out of sight. The intruder was up there, waiting for him, playing with him.

"I'm coming up!" Jeremy announced before he took the first step, a lump forming in his throat.

He stomped up the steps, his boots thudding loudly against the spiral staircase. The door to the lantern room was closed. He hesitated for a moment, wondering if the stalker was just on the other side, waiting to get the jump on him. Jeremy's hand firmly clutched the steel pipe as he shoved the door open.

"All right, enough games!" he stormed inside, the pipe resting on his shoulder so he could swing it quickly enough if needed.

His head jerked around along with his flashlight, looking for the person. The lantern rotated past Jeremy, momentarily blinding him. The lantern room was empty, and so was the walkway outside. No, that couldn't be. Jeremy ran a circle around the lantern, looking away every time the bright light approached him.

He wasn't convinced. Someone was here, he was sure of it. He stopped in front of the door leading out to the walkway, the flashlight in his hand and the keys in his pocket switching places. He held the right key firmly, contemplating whether to go out there.

He knew what awaited him there, but he also knew that he wouldn't be able to calm down until he took a look. He had to know. The ease at which he came to that conclusion surprised him.

Ignoring the *thump-thump-thump-thump* of his heart, he stuck the key inside the door and turned it. The moment he opened it, strong wind and rain wafted into his face.

"Shit," he raised a hand in front to shield himself from the elements.

The turbulent waves were nothing like the calm ones he'd seen earlier that day. Lightheadedness sloshed behind his eyes like the water occupying the scenery before him.

It could have been rage preventing his phobia from taking over. It could have been something else. He didn't try to theorize what it was.

He shoved the keys inside his pocket, grabbed the edge of the doorframe, and stepped outside.

***

The floor of the walkway did a good job of keeping Jeremy's feet steady despite the abundance of water that covered it. Nevertheless, his steps were skittish and tiny like a toddler learning how to walk.

The rain up there was incongruously more violent than it was on the ground. Jeremy had to squint against the droplets as his hands traced the circular wall. His eyes were fixated down on his feet. At first, only his palm pressed the wall, then his forearm, then his entire arm. He was about to press his back against it and sidle instead, but he knew that looking onto the horizon would only make him dizzy.

The intruder's somewhere around here. He has to be. I saw him.

But how could he possibly be here, Jeremy? You locked the walkway. And the lighthouse, Doctor Martelle's voice justified, but Jeremy ignored it.

Doctor Martelle was wrong. Someone *was* here, and Jeremy was going to find them.

His brain raced to find a reason as to why the mysterious person would go all the way to the top of the lighthouse instead of just seeking shelter, but he couldn't find a solution. All his brain was able to come up with was: People can be unpredictable sometimes.

But he was sure of one thing. The intruder was here.

Except they weren't. He had run into the door again rather fast, the full circle around the walkway complete. There was no one there.

No. It can't be. It just can't.

Jeremy had seen it. He'd seen the silhouette as clear as day, appearing just as the light swept past it. It hadn't been his imagination. It just couldn't be.

Or maybe it was. Remember the story about the lighthouse being haunted?

Is that what it was? He was being messed with by the ghost of the guy who killed himself? He went for another circle, his steps more confident this time but still stilted. Before he knew it, his hand was no longer on the wall.

See? Something good is coming out of all of this. You're learning to conquer your fear. Doctor Martelle grinned his gummy smile in Jeremy's mind.

"Fuck off, Doc," Jeremy said to no one.

Another full circle, and he was still alone on the walkway. He ran a circle in the opposite direction this time, convinced that the intruder was playing around with him, avoiding him.

Nothing.

Jeremy hadn't realized how out of breath he was until he stopped at the door once more. His legs were shaking. Standing still made him wobbly again, so he quickly located the wall and planted his palm on it. That felt better.

The anger that had carried him like a surfing wave was all but gone, replaced by dread and a growing sense of hopelessness. Jeremy felt like crying.

Why? Why was this happening to him? Hadn't he suffered enough already? Was god so cruel as to continue testing him even after taking everything from him? Was it just a sick joke?

Okay, you win, you beat me, he wanted to say, but to whom, he didn't know. To god? To the intruder? Neither of them was listening. To them, Jeremy was a joke. A toy to have fun with before throwing it away.

On a whim, he looked at the railing. He didn't know what compelled him to push away from the wall and approach the thin, metallic handle, but he did.

His free hand squeezed the handrail, the palm of the other hand pressing into the metal. It was wet and slippery, inadequate for a firm grip. He looked over the edge, his head suddenly weighing a thousand pounds. His eyes fell on the colossal waves that bashed the cliffside of the lighthouse. Lightning electrocuted the air, momentarily illuminating the line where the sky and the water met on the horizon.

Jeremy was so high up. *So* high up.

He reckoned that if he fell, he would have just enough time to let his fear run rampant before he hit the waves at full velocity. Hopefully, he wouldn't feel a thing. The ideation of jumping no longer seemed so foreign. Just a few seconds of plummeting, and then it would all be over.

That's how most people who jumped off bridges died. Their heads hit the surface of the water hard, and at that height, it was enough to knock them unconscious. The water would do the rest. The victim would be lulled into a peaceful death.

Jeremy leaned farther over the railing until his head and chest were suspended above the deadly height. He imagined clambering to the other side of the railing, leaning forward, his hands gripping the handrail the only thing stopping certain death.

He could simply… let go. Then, it would no longer be in his hands. Everything would be gone. The pain, the stress, the drinking, the nightmares… it would no longer be his responsibility.

A slam nearby jerked him out of his stupor.

He looked toward the door of the lantern room that had shut from the wind. The door represented something higher, something more important than just an entrance to the lantern room. It was like the door represented the threshold that led back to the world of the living.

Jeremy turned to face the vast ocean in front of him. The suicidal ideation was gone. What the hell was he thinking? He wouldn't have jumped, no. But just the fact that he had entertained those thoughts, even for a moment, was terrifying.

With the moment of clarity came the phobia, more powerful than ever, slamming into Jeremy like a train, like painkillers whose effects had worn off. He felt like puking when his eyes fixed on the waves far below. He pushed himself away from the railing and—

His foot slipped, sending him flying sideways. His shoulder hit the metallic floor hard, knocking the wind out of him, the steel pipe dropped out of his hand. It clattered on the walkway before falling over the edge. Jeremy's head hung over the edge. He watched helplessly as the steel pipe flew toward the water, growing smaller and smaller in size.

He was wrong.

It wasn't high up. It was *extremely* high up.

The waves didn't swallow the pipe until it was merely a toothpick in the distance. And then it was gone, forever lost out of sight in the infinite depths of the ocean.

Jeremy let out a yip as he scrambled away from the edge, his hands slipping on the watery surface. His eyes fell on the door, which bolstered him. He crawled to it, frenetically fumbled with the knob until it was open, and fell through the entrance before scooting backward until his back hit the lantern casing.

***

He was breathless. His heart threatened to explode from the beating, and his entire body felt brittle. This was a stupid idea. He shouldn't have come here at all. The anger that boiled in his skull made him want to cry out. He redirected it on the door by slamming it shut and locking it, telling himself he would never go out there again, no matter what kind of an emergency it was.

Even the lantern room no longer felt safe in terms of height. Jeremy crawled to the stairs, and only then did he remember the intruder. That problem was far at the back of his mind, barely a minor concern now. There was no way some hobo could do to Jeremy what his acrophobia did.

Right now, he only cared about one thing—getting the fuck out of the lighthouse.

His feet clobbered down the steps, echoing in the emptiness of the stairwell. He was at the bottom of the lighthouse before he knew it. He burst through the door and was back outside.

The cold rain that trickled onto him felt so good. The solid ground under his feet felt even better. The waves that lapped the pathway roared every time they crashed over the rocky surface, but the danger they posed was insignificant compared to the walkway above the lighthouse. It was like switching from an Olympic pool to a kiddie pool.

Jeremy shut the lighthouse door, locked it this time, and booked it down the path leading to the house. While skipping from rock to rock, his mind replayed the scene in which he'd seen the person on top of the lighthouse. Now that he thought about it, maybe it was all just his imagination. It easily could have been a trick of the light.

That made him feel a little better, but other thoughts were there to push him back down. Like blindly storming into the lighthouse, disregarding the possible dangers. Like jumping off the top of the lighthouse.

He didn't want to think about those things because he felt like his sanity was draining with each passing second.

The ocean wave that licked his legs and sent icy daggers through his shins sobered him up. He dashed the remaining distance to the house and crashed through the door. Tentative serenity lulled his body. He was away from the lighthouse, away from the blasted heights, away from the bad weather outside, and that was enough for the moment.

Just as his fingers gripped the hoodie to throw it back, the familiar *khhh* of the radio filled the room.

But it wasn't coming from the shoe stand where he'd left it.

It was coming from the kitchen... where the muddy tracks led.

Chapter 12

"Talk to me, Jeremy. You still there?" Dannie asked.

All Jeremy could do was gawk at the distinct footprints leading into the kitchen. It was a surreal sight. Here he was, alone in the middle of nowhere—or at least he was supposed to be—and deeply imprinted footprints clearly not belonging to his rubber boots stood before him.

It was supposed to be an impossible sight. And yet it wasn't. The mud tracked toward the kitchen was clear evidence of that, and no matter how many times Jeremy blinked, they wouldn't go away. At the same time, something nasty tangled in his gut because, whatever was going on here, it was no longer just a game. Whoever had done this meant business.

Instinctively, Jeremy took a stealthy step forward, the flashlight gripped so firmly in his hand that his fingers hurt. The light fell into the kitchen, and he became vaguely aware that whoever was in there would be alerted to his arrival. They would have the upper hand.

"Jeremy. If you're there, pick up."

One foot in front of the other, Jeremy inched closer to the kitchen, the cone of the flashlight trembling violently. He couldn't steady it, no matter how hard he tried.

Forget it. Just turn around and leave. Get to the control tower. Screw this. Don't put yourself in such danger.

But no matter how much his flight instinct screamed at him, Jeremy couldn't help but move forward. He was working on autopilot. Whether it be his lighthouse keeper's instinct or an otherworldly force, he felt compelled to do as it commanded.

"Jeremy? Don't do this to me. I can't get in touch with HQ right now, so I can't send help."

Jeremy peeked into the kitchen, the light bathing the table, casting elongated shadows that crept and refracted on the wall behind.

What small part of Jeremy believed that he was imagining the whole thing dispersed like bubbles popped by a needle when his eyes fell on the kitchen table. It wasn't a figment of his imagination. It was real. *Real.* And that meant that the threat he was facing was real, too. And whether he liked it or not, he had to face it because no one else was there to help him.

The thought of that made nausea seize his stomach. It made his hands and knees quiver. It made his throat ache with a dryness that only one kind of liquid could quench.

"Jeremy?" the radio spoke from the kitchen table.

It stood upright, facing Jeremy like a mockery of a gift left for him in an obvious place to find. He looked at the radio, but he also looked past it. The radio, as dangerous as it was, was not the real threat.

The real threat was the person hunkered behind the kitchen table where the mud tracks ended.

The light in Jeremy's hand was trained on the spot where the figure crouched, the shadows behind dancing tantalizingly. Here he was, standing mere feet away from the intruder.

Each was aware of the other's presence, no doubt about it. But what would happen next? Would the intruder attack Jeremy out of panic? Would he throw his hands up and plead with Jeremy not to hurt him? Would Jeremy see the same fear on his face as the one he himself felt? Would they both talk it out like two human beings, understand that it was all just a big misunderstanding, and sit down to drink one together?

The thought of the intruder being as afraid of Jeremy as Jeremy was of him gave him a whiff of reassurance. It also gave him a surge of much-needed confidence that he knew exactly where the intruder was. As long as he had his eyes on him, the person wouldn't be able to get the drop on him.

"Jer?" Dannie's voice was a nuisance. A distraction. An obstacle.

Jeremy slightly bent his knees, every muscle in his body tensing up. He dropped into a crouching position, the light of his torch bathing the underside of the table and revealing—

Nothing.

No one stood there. No ragged, gaunt figures crouching with their heads hanging down. Nothing but the mud tracks that abruptly ended behind the chair in an uneven streak, as if the person dragged their feet and then just disappeared.

They might have taken off their shoes. That's the only explanation.

Jeremy straightened his back, suddenly feeling way more vulnerable than moments ago. If the intruder wasn't there, then he could be anywhere in the house.

He could be watching you as we speak.

Jeremy spun around. He expected to see a face with long, greasy hair peeking behind the corner of the kitchen.

"Jeremy!"

"What?!" Jeremy's thumb dug into the PTT button.

"There you are. Where the hell have you been? I talked for well over five minutes." There was no accusation in Dannie's voice; only relief.

"Outside. Went to check if anyone was out there." Jeremy looked down at the mud tracks again, just to make sure he followed them right. They went from the foyer to the kitchen table, and that's where they ended. They didn't split anywhere along the way.

"And was there?" Dannie asked.

Jeremy poked his head toward the living room. "What?"

The living room was empty at first glance. He checked behind every piece of furniture.

"Was there anyone out there?"

"No," Jeremy said after a moment of hesitation.

But someone's inside with me, he wanted to say, but the only thing that stopped him from doing so was the fact that he didn't know if the intruder was listening. He wanted him to think that Jeremy was oblivious to him. He wanted him to let his guard down.

"See? There's no way anyone would be out there during this storm," Dannie said, a pang of *I told you so* in her timbre.

"Yeah."

Jeremy peeked into the bedroom. Nothing. He got on all fours and illuminated the space under the bed. Just prominent specks of dust. He yanked open the wardrobe and stepped back. The clothes strung on hangers stood motionless. The scowling red bull at the front of the sweater that stood atop the neatly folded pile silently asked "what the fuck is wrong with you" with its glower.

"Just my luck that the first night on the job gets this packed with action. But I have to say: This is kind of exciting, isn't it? It kind of reminds me of my first day as an EMT. It was a night shift, and..."

But Jeremy stopped listening. He stood in front of the service room door, staring at the doorknob glistening from water.

Looking farther down, he noticed droplets drying on the floor.

This was it. The fucker was in here.

"...and I had no idea what I was supposed to do, you know? But luckily, James was there to assist me, and..."

Jeremy retreated into the foyer, his eyes fixed on the service room door. He put the radio on the shoe stand and let Dannie do her talking. He then tip-toed to the door, the beam of the flashlight pressed against his stomach to muffle the light.

Jeremy stopped in front of the door, his free hand gently closing around the knob. It was slick and wet to the touch. He squeezed the knob harder. Dannie's receded speaking perforated the air from the foyer. Jeremy scrunched his lips.

The intruder wouldn't know what hit him.

Jeremy twisted the knob and shoved the door open, his flashlight penetrating the darkness of the room and swiveling spastically in every direction.

Empty.

No, that couldn't be right. Jeremy flipped the light switch on, his eyes darting around every corner of the room. Nothing. And it wasn't like the intruder had anywhere to hide in there. Aside from the panels on the wall, a single workbench occupied the room, too wide and tall to hide under without being noticed.

Jeremy spun in circles, refusing to accept that no one was inside. Someone *was* inside the house. They had to be.

The room buzzed with the electronics occupying it. Only then did Jeremy realize that the radio had gone silent in the foyer. He made a one-eighty on his heel and loped out of the room. Dread crept up on him as he approached the radio, thinking he would find it gone again.

It was right where he left it this time.

"Dannie?" he called to her.

Silence. Why was there silence? Why was she not ans—

"Still here," she replied after what felt like an eternity.

"Someone's definitely here." The words came out as blended, a quick recital.

"What?"

112

"Someone's inside the house. I'm sure of it." He turned so that he had a good view of the entrance into the kitchen and the living room. There was no way he'd let the intruder get the drop on him.

Dannie's response was delayed. "Are you sure? I mean, you said you checked—"

"I'm sure. Someone's tracks are inside. And when I returned from the lighthouse, the radio was not where I left it."

Dannie didn't respond. Jeremy held the radio up to his ear, waiting for her to say something. To say what, though? That he was just imagining things and that there was no way someone was in there with him? Part of him wanted to hear exactly that, but somehow, he knew that it would also anger him. He knew that someone was in the house, and he didn't need anyone to try to convince him he was crazy.

But what if Dannie confirmed his suspicion? What if she told him to not panic and get out of there? What if, when she spoke, Jeremy detected genuine concern in her voice for his safety; safety that she couldn't guarantee, no matter what she said?

But Dannie didn't reply to Jeremy's last sentence. He knew she was listening. He couldn't tell how, he just knew it. It was like hearing a person holding their breath on the phone. And then he realized; she was looking for the right words.

"You don't believe me," he said dryly.

"I never said that, Jer."

Jer.

It was what Nadine used to call him. He used to love that nickname, but only when she called him that. It was a nickname for him used only by her. But then he'd learned to despise the name. Whenever he was in situations where people aloofly called him Jer, he would correct them by simply saying, "Jeremy."

Hearing Dannie call him that didn't help alleviate the anger that had been building up toward her. He gritted his teeth hard, his jaw muscles aching from the effort.

"Okay, look," she said. "Why don't you check the entire house?"

"I already did," he said in a clipped voice.

"Let's do it again. Keep the radio on you and inform me as you clear each room. Okay?"

Jeremy sighed, his face somersaulting from grimace to grimace. In the end, he knew that Dannie was right. Whether he liked it or not, he had to check the entire house once more. Otherwise, he wouldn't be able to sleep.

"Jeremy?"

Jeremy locked the front door and scratched his forehead. He swallowed through a dry throat. He needed a drink so bad. "Okay."

***

"See anything?" Dannie asked.

"No. There's no one in the living room." Jeremy peeked behind the couch and then spun in a circle, giving the room another once over.

"Okay, you're doing good, Jeremy. Can you move to the next room?"

"Yeah."

Jeremy smelled patronization in Dannie's voice, but he ignored it. It was the least of his worries right now.

The door to the bedroom was open, the lights on. He peeked inside, the radio clutched firmly in his hand, the PTT button squeezed so that he could speak on short notice. "Bedroom's empty, I think."

"Good. Check every possible hiding spot, Jeremy. Under the bed, in the closet, behind—"

"I know," he interrupted.

114

This time, he made sure to swipe his hand through the wardrobe just to make sure nothing was ducking in there. The only thing his fingers came in touch with was the fabric of the hanging clothes.

"Talk to me, Jeremy. What are you looking at?"

"It's empty. The bedroom is empty."

"Great. Next up is the bathroom, right?"

"Yeah."

The bathroom was empty, too. And so was the service room. Something about the service room bothered Jeremy beyond words. He walked around the place, checking every nook and cranny. "No one's here."

"Good. Keep going."

Unlike the first time around securing the house, Jeremy was a lot calmer this time. Dannie's company soothed his nerves effectively, even if she was in reality some distance away and the object in his hand only a tool to transfer her voice and give him a false sense of security.

He hated being dependent on someone else. Ever since his divorce, he'd clammed up hard. People had tried approaching him, but they ended up giving up after a while. That worked for him. He didn't want anyone getting close.

But then there was Dannie.

He'd known her for less than twenty-four hours, and she was already making his walls crumble without even trying. Jeremy had built inner walls, too, but he didn't like the idea of anyone being able to breach even the outer ones.

"How many rooms are left?" she asked.

"Just the kitchen." He stepped out into the hallway and ambled in the direction of the final unchecked room.

"Okay, good. Let me know if you see anything. I'm here, okay?"

"Yeah."

Jeremy knew that there was nothing she could do if there really was a threat in the house. She was miles away, and even if she could call for help, which she couldn't because of the raging storm, it would be hours before they'd arrive. Jeremy could be dead ten times until then.

"I'm stepping into the kitchen now," he said into the radio.

It was the only room where the lights weren't on. Jeremy relied on his flashlight instead. He took a step inside and slowly pivoted the flashlight from right to left. His gaze briefly fell on the now-dry mud tracks that dirtied the kitchen floor.

"Do you see anything?" Dannie asked.

Jeremy's heart hammered in his chest, the pulsating spreading all the way up in his neck and ears. In the silence that clung to the air, he could hear his own rapid breaths.

"It's empty," he finally said.

The relief was audible in his breathless voice.

"Good. See? Everything's okay."

Jeremy lowered the flashlight, feeling a weight dropping off his shoulders. He wanted to laugh out loud from the relief that hugged him.

That was until his eyes fell on the open whiskey bottle on the counter.

CHAPTER 13

The moment of respite was gone, replaced by a dread stronger than he'd felt that entire night. As he stared at the bottle of brown liquid in front of him, Jeremy felt like a mouse being toyed with. It wasn't just the liquor bottle, either. A small bottle of pills lay toppled next to the whiskey, the pills spilled on the counter. The pills he kept in his bedside drawer.

He spun around the room, dread stirring with something that boiled at a high temperature.

Anger.

It took him over without any warning. Jeremy spun around and walked out of the kitchen, his fists clenching and unclenching. "Show yourself, you piece of shit!"

"Jeremy?" Dannie's concerned voice mixed in with his shouting, but it sounded as though it had come from the other side of a long tunnel.

Jeremy hadn't realized that his thumb was on the PTT button until then. He must have sounded like a lunatic to Dannie, but he didn't care about that in that moment. All he cared about was finding the intruder, pummeling the shit out of him, and tossing him out the door.

"He's in here, Dannie!" he said, indignation lacing his voice.

"Jeremy, you checked the entire house. You said you checked every roo—"

"Come out, damn you! Because if I find you, I swear to god, I'll kill you!" Jeremy stampeded through the living room.

Dannie's shouts and warnings fell on deaf ears. He was unaware of them. She didn't matter. Nothing mattered except finding the scumbag that had invaded the house—

his house. He stormed from room to room, looking through every possible hiding spot, shouting at the intruder to show his cowardly face.

When he found no traces of anyone inside the house, he unlocked the front door and stepped out into the rain. "I know you're here!"

He could hardly hear his own voice over the weather. Thunder was his response to the shouts along with Dannie's voice relentlessly begging him to calm down. With the words yelled out, Jeremy's shoulders drooped. It was as if the shout expelled the rage through his mouth, and without it, sudden vulnerability crept in on him.

"Jeremy. Please, answer me," Dannie pleaded, her voice tenuous.

Jeremy just then realized how stupid of him it was to walk out of the house so blindly. He wasn't thinking straight. His anger got the better of him. As he looked down at the murmuring radio in his hand, he realized that he should have listened to Dannie from the start.

Another crack of lightning.

With the rage deflating, the feeling of uncertainty swelled, and the profound need to get inside the house overtook him. He spun and ran back inside, making sure to lock the door tight. The silence of the house made him feel no better. He could no longer tell where he would be safe and where not.

The lighthouse. Get to the lighthouse.

"Jer, please," Dannie said.

"I'm here. I'm fine, for now," Jeremy said.

His voice sounded out of steam, exasperated.

"Thank God." Dannie sighed in relief. "Okay, tell me what's going on, Jeremy. What do you see?"

"Someone's here." Jeremy stopped at the living room entrance and scanned it.

118

"Who is? Do you see anyone there?"

"No. Not yet."

"Have you seen anyone?"

"No."

"Okay. So, how do you know someone's there, then?"

Jeremy knew how this all sounded. To Dannie, he must have seemed like a crazy person. A lone lighthouse keeper who finally lost it after months of solitude. But he wasn't crazy. He knew that someone was in there, and he had proof of it.

"The whiskey," he said to Dannie.

He ambled into the kitchen, ignoring Dannie's confused questions. Only when he saw the open whiskey bottle on the counter, proving that he was right all along, did he reply to Dannie. "There's a bottle of whiskey on the counter. It's open. Whoever was in here, he drank from my... he drank the whiskey."

"Jeremy..." Another sigh followed, this one coated with exhaustion.

Before Dannie could give him a lecture, he interrupted her, "I'm not going crazy. Okay? I always keep the whiskey inside the cabinet. And now it's... it's here. And the pills... They're always inside my nightstand drawer. I have never once taken them into the kitchen."

He gestured to the bottle as if it would help Dannie see it. He turned on the kitchen lights and approached the counter. The cap stood next to the bottle.

"Jeremy, just think for a moment," Dannie's worried tone came through. "You're out in the middle of nowhere, far away from anything resembling civilization. The control tower where I am is the closest place you have to human contact, and that's *miles* away. There is no way anyone would go all the way out there just to mess with you. It just doesn't make sense."

119

"You're wrong. Someone *is* here." Frustration hammered Jeremy's temples. Why wouldn't Dannie listen to him? The urge to close his hand around the neck of the bottle and chug was strong—so strong that Jeremy's hand shook like whenever he didn't eat for the whole day. "Earlier, the lighthouse door just opened on its own."

"Okay. So?"

"And when I went inside and climbed upstairs, the newspaper from the living quarters was on the kitchen table. The *kitchen* table!"

"I'm not following."

"I am sure that I left it on the coffee table. I'm sure of it. I remember because… because…" He closed his eyes, thinking hard, trying to retrace his steps. He snapped his fingers. "That's right, I left the window open. And when I returned, it blew the papers everywhere. I had to pick them up from the floor. And I distinctly remember putting them on the coffee table. I'm sure of it."

"Jeremy—"

"And then the front door just burst open on its own. It has never happened before, even during storms!" Jeremy walked out to the foyer and stared at the door as if it would shrug and confess to him that he was on to something. Dannie didn't respond. "And I saw a figure on top of the lighthouse! He was just standing there, staring down at me!"

Dannie remained silent.

"And then there's the message from HQ! Are you going to just ignore that, too?!"

Lock your doors, and stay inside.

At the time, Jeremy had thought it was because of the storm. But the message was vague. *Ominous.* As if he and Dannie should expect something far more terrible than a stupid storm.

120

Lock your doors. Stay inside.

Had they known that a dangerous individual was on the loose? Why didn't they tell Jeremy and Dannie anything about it? Perhaps to prevent panic? But Dannie had said that they'd sent that message a while ago, and it only later went through. Who was to say that they didn't send more messages after that, which didn't get through, either?

Lock your doors and stay inside.

There's a dangerous individual on the loose.

Police are on the way.

"Jeremy, just listen to me." Dannie's voice snapped Jeremy out of his reeling thoughts. "Have you been drinking tonight?"

The question cleaved at Jeremy. For a second, Dannie sounded like his ex-wife.

"What?" was all he could ask, dumbstruck and offended. He was out of breath. "Why would you say something like that? You think I wouldn't remember drinking?"

"I'm on your side, Jeremy. I just want you to try to remember when was the last time you drank, that's all." Dannie strangely sounded like an operator on the job trying to calm down a suicidal person.

Despite the anger, Jeremy relented. He thought back to earlier that day when he'd had a panic attack. He had opened the cabinet, he'd touched the bottle, he had closed the cabinet.

Or had he? Had he only touched the bottle? He squeezed his eyes shut and tried to imagine a scenario in which he took out the bottle, screwed off the cap, popped a few pills into his mouth, and washed them down with whiskey. The scene came to his mind with surprising ease. The longer he thought about it, the more both scenarios seemed likely—one where he was strong enough to resist the urge to drink and close the cabinet, and the one where he gave in to the temptation and sipped, even if just a little.

Then there was that dream, that's right! The one from earlier, when he walked up to the cabinet and washed the pills down with whiskey. Wait, had it been a dream? He had been sure of it, but now, faced with the sight on the counter...

"I..." he said, his sentence trailing off. "I can't remember."

"It's okay, Jer. It's all right."

Jeremy focused on the brown liquid. He tried to remember how full the bottle had been when he opened the cabinet earlier that day. That afternoon, the level of brown liquid had reached up to the shoulders of the bottle. Now, it was slightly under them.

The harder Jeremy thought, the more his head hurt. The more his thirst grew. The paradox of the cycle wasn't lost on him. He couldn't remember if he wasn't strong enough to resist the drink, and that itself made him want to drink.

"I... I opened the liquor cabinet today," he said.

"Okay," Dannie flatly said.

There was no sign of the judgment that he expected to hear in her tone. That encouraged him to speak up. "I don't remember. I... maybe I... I can't remember."

"It's okay, Jeremy. You're fine. It's perfectly normal to suffer relapses from time to time. The greater the improvement, the greater the relapse. You know?"

The way Dannie spoke about it made it sound like she knew he had a drinking problem. She probably did. How, though? He hadn't opened up that much.

Oh, but you did. Surprisingly, it was Doctor Martelle's voice that spoke in his head. *You see, when we speak to people, we inadvertently reveal more than we intend. We don't need to*

122

say outright that we're psychopaths, or racist, or gay, or that we like dressing up. It just sort of slips between the lines. And some people are good at noticing those things.

Dannie must have been really good at reading people. Or maybe Jeremy was that obvious. Perhaps five months of not interacting with another human being made him drop his guard. Perhaps a part of him *wanted* Dannie to get to know him. Maybe he needed someone to get close to him because he needed the comfort of someone telling him everything was going to be okay.

But everything was not going to be okay. He knew that. He'd known that for a long time now, ever since that call from the school.

Jeremy sniffled. His vision became blurry. It took him a moment to realize that it was tears that blurred it.

"But maybe... maybe it wasn't me... it... the intruder..." Jeremy said, the sturdiness of his voice barely hanging by a thread.

"Jeremy." Dannie's tone was stern now, like a parent trying to have a serious talk with a child. "There's no one there. You're alone there. Okay?"

Crying would be so easy. Jeremy could give in to the pain, and a sobbing fit would take over, powerful enough to incapacitate him for hours. He didn't want to let that happen. He'd spent so long building the dam that kept his fears and emotions behind it, and he wasn't about to let it all collapse over one incident.

Jeremy sniffled again, wiped his eyes until they were dry, and took a few deep breaths. Finally, he'd come to realize what the real danger had been. The threat that had plagued him the entire night hadn't come from an external source. It had come from him, and only him.

Jeremy ran a hand down his face while cold sweat formed on the nape of his neck.

A part of him still refused to believe alcohol had caused him to behave like this. He swallowed, trying in earnest to detect any lingering taste of the whiskey. He thought he could feel the remnants of the liquid in his mouth, mixed with saliva, but the harder he tried to pinpoint it, the more it evaded him, like trying to get food unstuck from between teeth.

Shame swaddled him. He had been too weak to resist the drink. It made him want to punch himself in the face. But more than that, fear wormed down his spine. He couldn't remember drinking, and that terrified him.

Was this the first time it happened? What if he thought he'd been doing okay while, in reality, his brain suppressed the memories of drinking bouts to make him feel better about himself? What if Dannie hadn't come along? Would the entire liquor cabinet be empty by the end of his shift?

He'd had enough. It was a familiar feeling. Whenever he woke up with a hangover, he told himself he would stop drinking. That would only last him until the hangover passed. But this was different. This time, he'd truly grown sick of it.

His drinking was spiraling out of control. What was next? Being driven to the ER because he couldn't control himself? He had already lost too much because of his alcohol.

And even as he thought about it, that persistent thirst wouldn't release its claws on him. Jeremy desperately needed a drink. He stared at the whiskey bottle, its promise of oblivion just at the tip of his fingers. Jeremy's hand hypnotically reached toward the bottle. His fingers closed around it, the cold feeling so, so good. He raised the bottle, feeling its weight in his hand.

Then, before he could change his mind, he brought the bottle to the sink and turned it upside down. The stream of liquid poured down the drain with a watery *gulp-gulp-gulp*, the bottle growing more and more transparent—it was draining so painfully *slow!!*—until the brown substance was completely gone.

He dropped the bottle into the sink, opened the liquor cabinet, and then began to uncap the bottles, one by one, with jittery hands, emptying them into the sink.

Stop! It's still not too late! There's still some left! Just stop!

He ignored the voice in his head. Caps flew around the kitchen as he unscrewed them and they flew off the bottles. Alcohol invaded his nostrils, calling to him, begging him to take just a lick, if not more.

When he emptied the final bottle, he dropped it on the pile in the sink and hurried out of the kitchen before he could change his mind and do something humiliating, like salvage the liquid from the sink. He would regret it hard later, he was sure of it. Right now, though, he was clear-headed (somewhat), and he knew this was the right choice.

He ran out of the kitchen and stopped in the middle of the living room, dazed and disoriented.

"I, uh…" Jeremy said to the radio but then trailed off.

"Yes?" Dannie asked.

"I… I think I fucked up."

He had to swallow and take in a deep breath to stop his voice from wobbling.

"Don't be so hard on yourself. You're only human."

"Yeah, but this is…" He shook his head, the thought of not remembering drinking surging through him like a sharp pain.

"Look, I know what it's like, okay? I know."

Something about that sentence bore significance, but Jeremy couldn't yet comprehend why.

"What do you mean?" he asked.

A deep sigh erupted from the radio. "I haven't been fully honest with you."

An anchor tugged at Jeremy's gut. The small amount of heat that remained in his hands and feet drained as he waited for Dannie to explain what she meant. A million things raced through his paranoid mind, but before he could properly entertain them, Dannie responded.

"I didn't quit my job as an EMT because I got sick of seeing the gore or because of the thing with David."

Jeremy waited with bated breath.

"I got fired."

Jeremy's gelatinous legs could hardly hold the weight of his body. He slumped down on the couch, his entire body weak from the stress. "Fired? What for?"

"It's… a long story."

Jeremy looked at his watch. A little past 11:30. The rain outside refused to stop. Lightning bellowed outside.

"We have a lot of time ahead of us," Jeremy said.

CHAPTER 14

"All right," Dannie responded. She didn't sound too thrilled to talk about a part of her life that she was obviously ashamed of.

Jeremy hated putting her in such an uncomfortable situation, but she was the one who'd mentioned it first. You don't just drop a bomb like that and then leave someone hanging. Besides, Jeremy desperately needed a distraction from the swirling emotions that ran like a tornado through a farm. He held the radio close, waiting for Dannie's story.

"After the whole thing happened with David, I got transferred to work in another hospital. I thought a fresh start would help me cope with the depression better."

"But you were wrong."

"Very. And things only seemed to get worse every day. I could hardly focus on anything. Then, one day, my coworker Barbara offered a little... pick-me-up. Since we worked in the hospital, it was easy to get a fix without raising suspicion. It was only supposed to be a one-time thing, you know?"

But it wasn't.

Jeremy understood that better than anyone. He could guess with surgical accuracy that things went down for Dannie the way they went down for him: Do it once, just to take the edge off, and you feel great. You wonder how you ever worried in life about anything. But then the pain comes back, and it somehow feels stronger. You need more of the magical painkillers to make it go away. By the time you realize it, you're addicted to the thing that takes the pain away.

Although the substance he used to numb himself was different, he and Dannie were the same. They were two people carrying unimaginable weight on their shoulders with no one to help them take a load off, looking for something to help them escape the prison that was their heads.

"How long have you been using for?" Jeremy asked.

"Oh, gosh. I stopped counting after the first year." Dannie nervously chuckled. "But considering I had worked there for three years and I had started using pretty much the month I arrived… there's your answer."

Jeremy bit his lip.

"I got too greedy, you know?" she said as if sensing that Jeremy was interested in the specific details. "I thought I'd never get caught because I'd managed to go so long without raising any suspicion. But then, one day, I took some, went back to work, and the next I knew, I was in a hospital bed with tubes attached to me."

"Jesus."

"Yeah. It was a close call. And naturally, the incident raised a lot of questions and prompted an investigation. It didn't take long for them to pinpoint where I got my fix from. I got fired and lost my license. My dad let me move in with him, but only if I promised to become clean. So, I did. I got a job as dispatch for Concordia Base, and when I found this, I transferred here. The pay's better."

"Just like that? I feel like you're skipping a step or two to the "become clean" part."

Dannie let out a hearty peal of laughter. "I had almost died when I OD'd. I was okay dealing with the grogginess and the excess amount of sleep. But when my life was on the line, it was like someone had flipped an invisible switch in my head, you know? No matter how hopeless I thought my life was, I didn't want to die. I guess survival instinct really is strong in humans."

"Not for everyone," Jeremy said.

The hand holding the radio drooped on the couch next to him. He looked at the blank TV screen and then at the window. He should have been sleepy, but instead, he was on edge. He felt like he wouldn't be able to fall asleep for hours. Not after everything that had happened tonight.

He was too thirsty. A glass of water stood on the coffee table. It had been there for two or so days now. Jeremy's body was too weak for him to walk all the way back to the kitchen and pour a new glass of water. Besides, demons awaited him there. He was afraid that even looking at the sink would cause his need for the booze to take control of him.

He leaned forward, cupped the glass in his hands, and drank the water in one big gulp. He slammed the glass back on the table and wiped his mouth just in time for the radio to come to life again.

"So, what about you?"

"What about me?" he asked, even though he knew what Dannie meant.

He was hoping to buy himself enough time to figure out an excuse as to why he shouldn't share his story, but no matter how much he hated it, it would only be fair to tell Dannie what she wanted to hear. After all, she told him about her dark secrets.

Jeremy wasn't afraid of other people knowing about the skeletons in his closet. He was afraid of talking about them because he didn't want to remember.

"When did it start for you?" Dannie asked in a solicitous inflection.

Jeremy let out a deep sigh. He didn't remember when exactly it had started for him. It had happened so gradually that the start was hazy. "Two years ago, I received a call from the school. It was about my son, Raymond."

He paused, carefully considering his words. It had been so long since he said his son's name aloud that it felt foreign.

"I thought you didn't have any family?" Dannie asked. Jeremy could imagine her eyes growing wide in terror at the realization before her next sentence, "Oh, Jeremy. No. Please don't tell me…"

"There was a school shooting. Ray didn't make it."

"Jer… I'm so sorry."

Maybe this was his cue to stop, but it was too late. The moment he opened that door was the moment the mound of forgotten trash seeped out like an avalanche, and he was powerless to stop it. Even after all this time, just uttering Raymond's name was a spell powerful enough to evoke the most painful memories of his life.

It had been a chilly fall Thursday, and he had been at work. He remembered clearly that he had been working at his desk on a report for a client. The day had been particularly busy: lots of emails, meeting requests, calls.

Jeremy had grown accustomed to answering his work phone without looking at the caller ID, so when his phone rang just before lunch, he thought it would be another client. The voice that had come through was deep and straightforward.

"Yes, this is Jeremy," he had said when the person on the phone asked him to confirm his identity.

Even after two years, he still remembered the first part of the phone call with the police as clear as day. He still remembered the police officer's somber tone when he had uttered the obviously rehearsed sentence.

Jeremy's mind had needed a moment to figure out what the person on the other end had said. All he had managed to register was "police" and "shooting." And then, like a rain-battered windshield cleaned by the wipers, the sentence crystallized.

130

"I'm calling from the police. I don't know how to tell you this, but... there's been a shooting at your son's school."

The words had hit Jeremy like a ton of bricks. His legs had cut off, so it was a good thing he had been sitting. A school shooting at Ray's school? The thought of that was absurd. Things like that couldn't possibly happen. Not to Jeremy and his family. No way.

And still, even as he conjured those thoughts, he couldn't stop his breath from going shallow, his temperature from dropping by twenty degrees, and the room from spinning.

Then the police officer delivered the final blow, "Your son didn't make it."

Those words stuck with Jeremy for many nights while he stared at the cracked ceiling of the living room. Sometimes, he thought he could hear the police officer's voice right in his ear as if it was there to remind him of his ultimate failure as a dad.

That was only one of the many things that had plagued him daily in the past two years.

Meeting Nadine at the school and seeing the look on her face was another. The look that told him she would never be the same. She would never be his wife again. All that would remain of the woman he'd shared his life with would be a hollow husk.

Then, there was the worst of it all—the what-ifs.

What if he had done something differently? What if he had told Ray not to go to school that day and, instead, they took a collective day off as a family and went to a theme park? What if Ray had picked different classes? What if Jeremy had simply *spoken* to Ray that morning?

That pained him immensely. That morning, he had been late to work, so he had gone downstairs to pick up the lunch that Nadine had prepared for him, kissed her on the

131

cheek, tousled Ray's hair while he ate his cereal, and went to work without a second thought.

The Jeremy who had left the house that morning had been worried about a stupid promotion. He didn't think, in his wildest dreams, that it would be the last time he'd see his family together.

The last time he would ever be happy in life.

"I didn't start drinking right away," Jeremy said to Dannie. "I didn't think about anything except the pain. When something like this happens to your child, you blame yourself. You wonder what you could have done differently to change the outcome. You wonder too late. So, all that's left to do is blame yourself."

He took a moment to compose himself. He let out a trembling breath before continuing, "Drinking came spontaneously. Nadine and I had grown apart quickly. We had become strangers. I needed something. I didn't know what, but I couldn't take living like that anymore; wallowing in what could have been, day after day."

"So, one day, I took a bottle of whiskey and decided, fuck it, I was going to drink the whole thing right there. It had been some time since I'd gotten drunk, but I'd never gotten blackout drunk before. When I woke up in the morning with a splitting headache, Nadine was there. She gave me this look… a look that said I was at the bottom, and I still managed to sink lower.

"I didn't care. Just wanted the pain to end, just for a moment, so I could take a break. I was tired. Raymond's death haunted me all day long, every day. I took sleeping pills just to escape the reality. But whenever I slept, I had nightmares. I wanted it all to end. So, I drank."

Jeremy was shaking. He hadn't realized it until he felt how much his thumb wobbled on the PTT button. He let it go, leaned forward, and rubbed his face to chase the heat from it. Talking about this all turned out to be somewhat easier than he thought it would be. He had already discussed this a million times over with Doctor Martelle, but he hadn't mentioned Raymond to a soul ever since he stopped going to therapy.

Until tonight.

"Nadine and I separated some time later. I found the divorce papers in my mailbox within a year. We kept in contact for a while, and I don't even know why. We just did, maybe because it felt like the right thing to do. The calls dwindled after a while, and... we sort of just stopped contacting each other."

Jeremy's head was killing him. Already, the alcohol hankering was setting in, but he was resolved to fight it. He blinked a few times, hoping to chase the nagging headache away. "You wanted to know my story. There you go."

"I cannot imagine how difficult it must be living through something like that," Dannie said with a motherly tone. "I'm so sorry, Jeremy."

It occurred to Jeremy what an awkward position Dannie was in. She had asked to hear Jeremy's story, and she got way more than she bargained for. Now, she probably felt obliged to say something to make him feel better, but she didn't know what.

He was about to offer to change the subject when darkness engulfed the entire house.

***

"What the hell?" he said, his thumb instinctively pressing the radio button.

He was stuck in complete and utter darkness, totally blind to everything around him.

"What's going on?" Dannie asked.

"The power just went out." Jeremy stood up.

He momentarily lost balance before assuming a stable stance.

"What? Can you see what caused it?" Dannie asked.

"Must be because of the storm." Jeremy put one hand in front of himself and blindly shuffled through the room.

His shin grazed the coffee table. The lighthouse came into view through the window. The lantern was still functional because it worked separately from the rest of the house. His hand brushed the nearby wall. He planted his palm on it and traced it along the wall toward the foyer.

There, he located the flashlight that he had left on the shoe stand. His heart skipped a beat when he couldn't find it, and his first thought was: The intruder had moved it just like the radio. The momentary fright disappeared the second the tip of his pointer jabbed the familiar object.

He wasted no time turning on the light. The beam of light that bathed the foyer was like his own personal lighthouse. With it in his hand, he felt a lot better. He strode into the service room, sweeping the cone past the blinking lights on the panels.

He located the fuse box separated from the panels and searched the top of the box for the triangular key. His fingers wiped a bunch of dust before they collided with the metallic object. Jeremy unlocked the fuse box and opened it, inspecting the damage.

He may not have been good with electricity, but he at least knew how to deal with fuse boxes because the old house used to have problems with power outages whenever too many utilities were active.

The problem in front of him was apparent at first glance, as soon as the box was opened.

One of the fuses was missing.

Chapter 15

All he could do was stare at the hollow socket where the fuse should have been inserted. He was met with another dose of surrealism like when he saw the radio on the kitchen table. Just like it, the socket in front of him shouldn't have been empty.

But it was. And no matter how many times he blinked, the sight didn't change.

The fuse was still missing.

His first instinct was to report the situation. "It's not the storm," he said curtly.

"How do you know?" The relaxed manner in which Dannie asked told Jeremy she didn't understand the severity of the situation.

"Because one of the fuses is missing." Jeremy closed the fuse box and turned around.

This entire night was a mess. The rollercoaster of dread, fear, and anxiety was unending. He couldn't take it anymore. He felt like he was going crazy.

"It's... missing?" Dannie asked.

"Yeah."

Here it comes, he thought to himself. *She's going to try to convince you that it's all in your head. That you're the one who took out the fuse.*

Jeremy braced himself for a rebuttal, but Dannie's response was worse than he expected because it didn't make him angry.

It sent a cold, unadulterated fear sparking through his torso.

"Jeremy, I want you to find a safe room to lock yourself inside."

That confirmed it. It was *real.* The entire thing had been real the whole time, but now that another living human had confirmed it, he knew just how real it was. And then a follow-up thought told him: *You're in danger.*

As if on cue, as if realizing that Jeremy had become aware of another person's presence in the house, a crash exploded in the kitchen.

Something shattered into pieces and was then proceeded by silence. Even the sound of rain seemed to retreat, making room for the unnerving quiet. Jeremy's flashlight was pointed at the door, a faint light cast on the hallway outside.

"Jeremy? Can you hear me?"

Jeremy brought the radio to his face but then paused. A muffled *thud-thud-thud-thud* reverberated in the walls as footsteps traveled through the house. Jeremy held his breath at the ensuing silence.

"Y-yeah. I hear you," he whispered.

"Do you have a place where you can hide?" Dannie's voice was too loud, too obtrusive against the silence that draped the house.

He muttered something that was supposed to sound like "I think so" but was barely audible, even to him.

"Okay, can you go there now?" Dannie asked.

"Yeah. I'll do it."

"Okay. Stay on the radio, okay? I'm going to try to contact the police, okay?"

Despite the calmness of Dannie's tone, that sentence sent a cold wave down Jeremy's spine. If the police had to be involved, then it really was a serious issue. At the back of his mind, he'd known that all along, but something had been stopping the full realization of it from surfacing.

Defense mechanism. You're already losing your mind, and your brain is trying to protect you.

Jeremy swallowed. His mind reeled as he tried to think of a safe place where he could hide. His first thought was the bathroom. He nodded in silent agreement and then focused on the hallway outside. He had to go out there in order to reach the bathroom.

That meant that he might run into the intruder on the way there.

Jeremy's foot moved automatically. He took one step forward, then another, until he was steadily inching toward the door. The torch in his hand trembled so badly that the beam looked like it was held by someone having a seizure.

He didn't want to prolong the suspense. The intruder probably already knew where he was, so why stall it? Jeremy strode the rest of the steps to the door and, before he could chicken out, poked his head out into the hallway, toward the kitchen.

The trembling of his hands grew stronger. His desire for something to calm down the tremor—say, a bottle of whiskey—was powerful.

A clatter from the living room caught his attention.

He couldn't see the living room from here, but the loud shuffling and scraping noise that came from it had Jeremy imagining the intruder dragging something heavy across the ground. The noise came at a clipped *skrrrp*, *skrrrp*, *skrrrp*, before stopping entirely. Then something else clanged on the floor.

Jeremy tip-toed down the hallway. His brain raced to scenarios and solutions on how to reach the bathroom safely. The entrance to the living room was directly across from the bathroom, so he would need to be fast.

Silence engulfed the house once more. As unnerving as the noise was, the silence was worse. It was like waiting for something horrible to happen: perhaps a loud, startling sound.

He stopped at the edge of the entrance to the living room, his flashlight pointed down, his breaths shallow and suppressed. Three heavy footsteps stamped in the living room. Then some rustling took over. What the hell was the intruder doing?

Jeremy's eyes were fixed on the bathroom door. It was right there, just a few feet away from him. He bent his knees, his entire body tense and ready for a sprint.

Then, the silence was broken by an obnoxiously loud noise. A noise that didn't come from the living room. A noise that put Jeremy on the radar of whoever was in there with him.

The radio produced a loud *khhh* before Dannie spoke up. But Jeremy didn't listen to what she said because it was drowned out by the sound of glass shattering in the living room.

Jeremy bolted to the bathroom. The footsteps from the living room came after him, heavier than before. *I'm going to murder you,* their aggressive stampeding said.

Jeremy barreled through the bathroom door with his shoulder and backhanded it with the side of his fist. The door slammed shut, and he propelled himself into it, his heels digging into the floor as he fumbled for the lock.

His fingers pinched and swiftly turned the lock with ease, just in time for something to slam against the other side. It wasn't a powerful whack, just enough to let Jeremy know that something real was on the other side of the door.

The doorknob rattled. Jeremy reflexively stepped away from the door, his eyes fixed on the jangling knob. Just as quickly as it started, the effort of trying to get in was over, leaving the bathroom in complete silence. Jeremy's flashlight gravitated to the crack beneath the door and the shadow that occupied it. Slowly, the silhouette shifted and then slinked out of view, followed by receding footsteps.

Only then did Jeremy allow himself to suck in a breath that his brain begged him for. His chest hurt from the adrenaline that seized him, and his legs felt like they were made of pudding. He collapsed onto the floor and leaned his shoulder against the wall, exhaustion enveloping him, his head throbbing.

He heaved in heavy breaths of air, allowing himself a moment to rest. Sweat coated his forehead. He wiped his forearm across it. Despite the close call, heaviness lingered on his eyelids, making him sleepy. Jeremy closed his eyes, just for a moment.

CHAPTER 16

Dannie's incoherent voice startled him. He looked at the door, somehow expecting it to be open, the intruder standing above Jeremy with a machete in his hand. The door was still firmly closed, but that did nothing to alleviate the worry and fear that cleaved his gut.

"Dannie…" he breathlessly said.

"Jeremy! Are you okay? Did you make it to a safe place?" she asked.

This time, the worry in her voice was palpable.

"Yeah. I locked myself in the bathroom. He's still out there. Did you manage to call the cops?"

"No. I can't get through."

Shit.

Jeremy squeezed his eyes shut, the throbbing in his head refusing to let go. He was stuck in the middle of nowhere with a potentially dangerous individual in the house… and no help on the way. He had no idea how this was going to play out.

"Are you safe in there?" Dannie asked.

"Yeah. I locked the door. But I don't know if he can get inside." Some of the words came out as a wheeze due to his breathlessness.

"Okay. Just stay in there. All right? I'll keep trying to contact the police. Just don't move from there, okay?"

"Yeah."

Jeremy refused to avert his eyes from the door. He expected the doorknob to start rattling again any moment, or banging to resound on the door, or—

Or a different sound. Perhaps the sound of an axe splintering the wood.

A jolt of panic passed through Jeremy like a supernova. There was an axe in the service room. If the intruder found it, he could easily break through the door. Jeremy would have nothing to defend himself with. Moreover, the only other way out of the bathroom was through the tiny window on the back wall—a window too small for Jeremy to squeeze into.

He was boxed in over there, cornered like a rat.

His chest tightened with panic. His throat closed up, allowing barely any passage of air. Was this what claustrophobia felt like? Did he score a new fear to add to the list? As if sensing his predicament, Dannie broke the silence. "Jeremy, how are you holding up there?"

"Not... not good."

"What's going on?"

"I'm locked in the bathroom. There's no other way for me to get out. If the intruder gets in..."

"Jeremy, hey. Listen to me. You're going to be okay. All right?"

But Jeremy sure didn't feel okay.

"Jeremy?" Dannie insisted.

"I..." Jeremy couldn't breathe.

"Stay calm, Jeremy. Let's talk, okay? What's your favorite dump of a place?"

"What?" Jeremy hyperventilated. The walls felt like they were closing in on him.

"Dump of a place that has a special place in your heart. What is it? Mine was Mike's Bridge Diner. What about yours?"

"Oh." Jeremy sighed, only just now realizing what Dannie was trying to say, but he couldn't focus because of the lack of air in the room. "Um..."

"Come on, Jer. You gotta have someplace that you like despite its shortcomings."

Jeremy closed his eyes and thought hard while trying to regain his breath.

"Hadlock Field," he expelled the words from his mouth.

"Hadlock Field. Okay," Dannie echoed. "Why Hadlock Field?"

"Ray and I... we used to go there to... to watch the Portland Sea Dogs games."

"Ray must have had fun."

"Yeah." Jeremy was able to heave in more air without having to strain so hard. "His mom wasn't a baseball fan, so it was just the two of us. It... it became a regular routine for us after a while. Just the two of us, eating hot dogs, watching the game, yelling at the players for not knowing how to play..."

"It doesn't sound like the place was a dump, though."

"It was." Jeremy chortled. "The field was unkempt. The seats were broken and dirty. Bubblegum, leftover food, spilled drinks... you could even see an occasional critter running between the seats. I even witnessed once a guy stabbing his arm on a sharp piece of a broken seat."

"Yikes."

"Yeah. They'd stopped investing in the field after a while. But Ray and I still loved it, so we were able to look past the mess."

"I don't need to ask if you still go there, right?"

"No. You don't."

Jeremy felt a little better after the talk. He no longer felt like he was suffocating.

"Jer? You're going to be okay, I promise."

Jeremy knew she couldn't make such a promise, but he fervently nodded nonetheless, even though Dannie couldn't see him.

"What I want you to do is look for something in there to defend yourself. Okay? Can you do that?"

"Yeah. Hold on, let me look." Jeremy used the supporting wall to clamber up to his feet.

The reflection in the medicine cabinet mirror that stared back at him was ghastly. His hair was a disheveled mess, his cheeks sunken, his skin pallid, his eyes wide with fear. Unable to bear the sight of the phantom he'd become, Jeremy opened the medicine cabinet and rummaged through the items, not caring that he was swiping half of them into the sink on the floor.

"I can use scissors. I have a pair of scissors here," he said.

"Good. Anything else?"

Jeremy put the flashlight on the sink and gripped the scissors firmly in his hand, trying to feel the handle on them. He grasped the object firmly and gave it a test thrust. He tried to imagine what it would be like for the pointy ends to sink into human skin. Would they be sharp enough to hurt them?

They sure looked deadly enough. And if he managed to strike a sensitive spot, say, an eye…

The scissors in Jeremy's hand made him feel a lot safer. At least, he was armed with something. He remembered the guns he used to have back at home, and he thought about how he should have at least brought a revolver to this place, exactly for this kind of situation.

No, I would never use guns again. Not after…

"There's nothing else I can use. Just the scissors," he said.

"Okay. It'll have to do. How are you feeling?"

"What do you think?"

"Sorry."

The apology prompted Jeremy to consider something. It was Dannie's fault he was in this mess. She was the one who'd convinced him that it was all in his head. If she'd just let him find the intruder in time and deal with him, he probably wouldn't have been stuck in the bathroom now, a pair of scissors painfully clutched in his hand, his eyes fixed on the door in anticipation of when it would start rattling again.

The indignation toward Dannie that simmered in his gut was unbearable. He wanted to yell at her, tell her how it was all her fault, how he wouldn't be in this mess if she'd allowed him to do this thing.

But then a rational part of him prevailed. He couldn't possibly blame Dannie. This was all the intruder's doing. Besides, Dannie probably knew better than anyone how unreliable alcoholics and drug abusers were. She had firsthand experience.

Jeremy slid to the ground into a sitting position and ran a hand down his face. He was so tired all of a sudden. He just wanted morning to arrive.

"Jeremy?" Dannie called to him, but he didn't feel like talking.

The residual anger still clung to him like a persistent stain.

"I'm sorry," she said.

Jeremy frowned at the radio in his lap.

"I should have believed you," Dannie's voice came out as mournful. "I'm sorry."

He wanted to continue feeling angry, but he couldn't. He detected genuine regret in Dannie's words, and that was enough to disperse his anger.

"It's fine," he said. "I probably wouldn't believe a washed-out alcoholic, either."

"You're being too hard on yourself. This is not an everyday scenario."

"Maybe. But it still feels like all the odds are against me tonight."

"At least, it's not your first day on the job. If you die, it's probably going to look bad on my resume."

"Which is already pretty colorful from past experiences, I'm sure." A smile crept up on Jeremy's lips.

Dannie let out a peal of laughter. "Really, though. You'll be okay, Jer."

He found it strange how he got accustomed so quickly to Dannie calling him by that nickname.

"No one can guarantee that," he said.

"Well, my mom always said that things should be looked at from a positive perspective, not a negative one, especially when you're in a tough situation. The glass is half-full kind of thing, you know?"

"And how exactly do you do that?" Jeremy scoffed.

There was a delay before Dannie answered, "My mom always made milestones. Something to motivate her to get out of the dregs. Like, when she got interviewed for a new job, she said she'd take the whole family to Disneyland if she got the position."

"And did she?"

"No, but she got a different one. And we did go to Disneyland."

"Sounds like a fond memory."

Jeremy smiled. He thought back to the time he took his own family to Disneyland, back when Raymond was six. Seeing the smile on his son's face and hearing his genuine laughter made standing for hours in the waiting lines worth it. The trip also brought him and Nadine closer together.

He remembered thinking back then that Ray was going to grow up someday and move out, and he dreaded that time coming so soon. At the same time, he was also committed to enjoying his time watching his son grow and become his own person.

It never occurred to him that Ray—and Ray's parents—would be robbed of that future.

"Anyway, we need to give you an incentive to make it out alive," Dannie said.

"Okay, what?"

"Hm…" Dannie said. "If you survive, I'm buying burgers at Bentley's."

"Either you're setting the bar too low, or those burgers really mean a lot to you."

"You haven't tasted their burgers. They're… something divine."

Jeremy looked at the door. He wondered if the intruder could hear their conversation. He didn't care. He was tempted to look through the keyhole, but something was stopping him from doing so.

Fear.

He was afraid that looking outside, he would be met with the figure of the intruder standing in front of him, confirming that he was still inside the house. For all he knew, maybe the person had already left, but waiting until morning would still be the safest option.

"Hey, if you want, we can change the reward," Dannie said.

"I can't really think right now."

"Okay. Hey, you should stop by the control tower when your shift is over."

Jeremy carefully considered that. He enjoyed chatting with Dannie on the radio, but he wasn't sure if he wanted to meet her in person because that would add a whole new layer of responsibility—and he had trouble even with voice chat.

At the same time, he wondered what she looked like. It was only a passing thought, not sufficient enough to convince him to hop on a ride to the control tower. Besides, talking with someone on the radio and talking face to face were two completely different things. For all he knew, the air between him and Dannie would be awkward, and he wanted to avoid that if possible.

"Let's focus on making it through the night for now," Jeremy said, hoping it would be enough to close the subject.

It was.

Silently, he thought of his own incentive to get out. The thought of downing an entire bottle of whiskey was vastly tempting, and he was immensely disgusted with himself for even considering drinking again.

CHAPTER 17

For a while, silence loomed in the bathroom. Dannie was the one who broke that silence.

"You doing okay, Jer? You're awfully quiet in there."

"Oh, you know. Just worried that an axe murderer is right outside the door."

"We don't know if he's an axe murderer. Could be just a homeless person looking for some food."

"Maybe."

Jeremy didn't want to speculate anymore. It would only further drive him insane. He tried to think about living to see the next day. For a split second, he felt hopeful. But that hopefulness evaporated like water on a hot day.

The following day would be the same. And the one after that. And all the other days until the day he died. The truth was he died the day he received that phone call from the police.

That realization had been in front of him this entire time, and for some reason, Jeremy hadn't seen it. Perhaps he was clinging to something; some kind of hope that he would find something to pull him up from the muck and give him a reason to live.

So far, nothing like that came. Living day by day was like constantly being tired, but never able to fall asleep. And still, suicide was not an option. He didn't know why, it just wasn't. Perhaps it was the fear of eternal hell that held him back from it. No, there was no worse hell than the one he was living on this earth.

Jeremy had been raised as a catholic, albeit not an overly religious one. He went to church with his family on Sundays from time to time. He tried to stick to the rules written in the Bible, but that was pretty much it.

After the incident that changed his life, he remained a believer, and for a while, he questioned god over why things had to be the way they were. But then that morphed into anger, and hate.

He needed someone to blame, and he could blame himself only so long. So he blamed god. There was no way that a deity powerful enough to take an innocent child's life—and in such a cruel manner—could be good. For all Jeremy knew, it was all just a game for the big guy above—and the people living on the planet were expendable figures.

"We should talk to get your mind off things," Dannie said.

"Okay, about what?" Jeremy welcomed that suggestion with open arms.

"Hm... let's imagine what would happen if the roles were swapped. You give me your speculations, and I'll give you mine."

"Sure." Jeremy straightened his back as he carefully considered the scenario in which he was in the control tower and Dannie was the lighthouse keeper. He had difficulty imagining her living where he was, fixing things day after day for six months. "Well, let's see. You'd probably handle this better than me. You'd know right away that it wasn't you going crazy and that someone was really there. You seem like the kind of person who would run to the lighthouse, all the way up to the lantern room, and lock all the doors along the way."

"That... does sound like a good plan. And what would you do in the control tower?"

Jeremy narrowed his eyes. "If I were there and I couldn't get in touch with the police? Honestly, I'd equip myself with whatever I could find and go to the lighthouse."

He understood how the words sounded, but they'd already left his mouth. He didn't want Dannie to think he was blaming her for sitting in the control tower and not doing more because there wasn't anything more she could do. Coming to the lighthouse would only put both of them in danger, instead.

"Aw, you'd come rescue me?" she asked. "That wasn't the impression you left on me."

"What kind of impression did I leave?"

"I don't know. Rough, cold. Not giving a damn about other people."

"A little harsh, don't you think?"

"Have you heard yourself? You sound scary at times."

"That still didn't stop you from talking to me."

"Because I know there's something underneath that layer of toughness."

Jeremy ran a hand through his hair. Once again, he was overcome with the realization that the walls he'd worked so hard to put up were crumbling in front of Dannie. He knew it went both ways, and he didn't like it.

Still, curiosity got the better of him, so he asked, "How did you know?"

"Because we're polar opposites," Dannie said. "I'm cheerful and joke around all the time while you go all the way in the other direction. Those extremes always indicate that the person is hiding something that they don't want other people to see."

Jeremy considered that for a moment. He wondered if other people were able to see what Dannie saw. He didn't like that thought. He felt way too exposed, way too naked. Realistically, most people would give Jeremy one glance and think to themselves, "What is this asshole's deal?" but there were some people—people like Dannie—who were able to see past the initial impressions.

"Okay, so what's your verdict? Would I survive or die?" Dannie asked.

"We don't even know who I'm up against." Jeremy shook his head.

"Let's consider the worst, just for the sake of the game. Let's say that it *is* an axe murderer."

"Which it very well might be." Jeremy's tone lowered to a whisper.

Jeremy's eyes drifted to the door. It was still, just as it had been since he entered the bathroom. The house had been quiet as well. Maybe the intruder was already gone. He didn't want to peek, not yet.

"You sound tough. You'd probably live," Jeremy said.

"I don't know how right you are. I'm trying to imagine myself in that situation, and I think I'd run out of that house screaming, not even knowing where I was going. If it was an axe murderer, he'd probably catch up to me and cut me to ribbons. I mean, I'm a good runner, but not that good. Especially not under pressure."

"Hm," was all Jeremy said.

Dannie must have sensed that the topic wasn't making Jeremy feel any better, so she added, "Let's talk about something else. All this talk about axe murderers is just making me more anxious."

"Okay." But Jeremy couldn't think of anything to talk about. He held the radio up to his mouth, his thumb gently on the PTT button as his mind raced through all possible small talk scenarios.

For years, he'd used icebreakers with clients, and it went naturally for him. Asking them how their flight was, about the state they came from, showing interest by echoing what they said and talking about similarities in topics, etcetera.

But the ice had already been broken with Dannie. Asking her about her hobbies or favorite movies and music

153

felt too contrived. Then something did come to his mind. "What was it like working with White Mars?"

"Not as eventful as working here, I'll tell you that." Dannie scoffed.

"Tell me a little about the base."

"Let's see…"

Dannie proceeded to talk about White Mars in as many vivid details as she could. Jeremy closed his eyes and imagined a vast, white desert, perpetually silent, a gray sky looming above. In the middle of that desert would be a fenced-off area fit to classify as a small town, but instead of numerous residential buildings, heavy machinery and cranes and dome-shaped buildings would occupy the majority of the place.

Not too many people would be around, and those who were—they'd all be bundled into thick clothes that made them look like astronauts. It would be painfully cold there all the time. Taking a bottle of water out would cause it to freeze within seconds.

And what about the inside of the station?

Perhaps a dorm-like place where the employees lived, often dark because the sun wouldn't be out for long. Inside, the people would be able to walk around in their t-shirts and other light clothes without worrying about preserving their body heat. But even going out for a smoke break would require them to put on layers and layers of clothes.

"Have you ever thought about visiting the base?" Jeremy asked.

"God, no!" Dannie sounded offended. "I can't even stand winters in Maine. When I visit my sister in Canada, I'm always miserable. Concordia Station… I'd probably want to commit suicide."

Jeremy let out a chuckle. "Did you have a keeper who you talked to all day long there, too?"

154

"Concordia Station had an entire crew, but I really only kept in touch with the communications guys. Some of them were talkative, some were not. Really, not a lot had been going on there. The only time we talked about work-related stuff was when they needed me to relay something to HQ. Otherwise, it was chit-chat."

Jeremy shifted on the floor because his back was starting to hurt from the uncomfortable sitting position. He didn't respond to Dannie's remark because her sentence sounded cut off as if more was to come.

"There was one guy I used to talk to more than the others. His name was Caleb," she said.

There it was. A story lurked behind those words.

"Wanna tell me about him?" he asked.

More silence, but only because Dannie was bracing herself, thinking of a way to start the story, Jeremy realized.

"Caleb was pretty young. Twenty-two at the time. I remember thinking, the first time I talked to him, 'What is someone so young doing so far from home? But then he explained why he preferred White Mars over home?' Caleb had a tough life. He came from a poor, abusive family. He had trouble keeping a job until he landed the position in Concordia Station. He was happy with the pay, but he always talked about not wanting to stay there forever."

"Did he specify what he wanted to do?"

"Yeah. He wanted to join the military. But that was something he planned on doing in the distant future. He wanted to work on White Mars for at least a few years. But anyway, we talked almost every day since that's what comms people do. They talk. He was kinda flirty. I kept reminding him how much older I was, but that didn't stop him from throwing in some comments here and there."

"Did that bother you?"

"I liked it. I mean, it had been months since I dated, and the last date I'd had prior to starting work with Concordia Station was disastrous—the guy was a total tool. Either way, I was lonely, and because of everything that happened with David, I felt unwanted. So, to have a young guy like Caleb flirt with me… it was exactly what I needed."

Jeremy stared intently at the radio. Once again, he felt like Dannie wasn't telling him everything. Perhaps she was ashamed of admitting what really happened?

"Did anything ever… happen between you two?" he dared to ask, not wanting to be too direct.

"Well, some nights there could be lonely. It was just me and Caleb. And he often went into… topics that weren't work-related. So it got kind of steamy from time to time. I remember him telling me how he needed to take off some of his clothes because it was getting so hot in there." She let out a reminiscent chuckle and then quickly cleared her throat. "Oh God, you must think so badly of me now."

"No. I don't," Jeremy said. He could go into explanations about why it was completely okay for Dannie and Caleb to have an intimate relationship, but he felt that voicing it would kill it, so he just left the sentence at what it was.

"Well, things didn't stop there. He and I exchanged pics, and he said he would like to meet me when our shifts were over. I was reluctant at first because what could possibly go on between me and a fifteen years younger kid? Because that's what he still was, a kid, no matter how mature he was."

"But you didn't see him as a kid?"

"No. I mean, I did at first, until I didn't. And then these feelings toward him started to form, and I hated myself for it. Anyway, I agreed to meet with him. I gave him my number and told him to call me once he was back in the States." At this point, Dannie let out a deep sigh. "I waited

156

for his call, but it never came. Weeks passed, and my shift started again. By then, I had gone through all these different scenarios in my head, and I figured that Caleb must have changed his mind. I was kind of hurt, but I also understood his side. Like I said, I was much older than him. Still, I was impatient to go back to work and talk to him, see what was going on. I was far too invested in this radio relationship of ours, you know?"

"I get it," Jeremy said.

"But when I got back, Caleb was no longer there. I waited for his shift, but there was a new guy instead there. I asked the other comms guys where Caleb was, but no one seemed to know. All they knew was that Caleb no longer worked on White Mars."

Jeremy gulped. He sensed something bad upcoming.

"I did some digging, but I couldn't get any concrete information. The company was strict about the privacy of their employees and whatnot, so I couldn't get any information. When my shift there was over, I went to HQ and stormed into the boss's office, demanding to know what had happened to Caleb."

Jeremy detected shakiness in Dannie's voice. She was also speaking a little faster.

"It took me a while to convince him, but eventually, he pulled up a news article online. Caleb and his friends got drunk and had gone for a ride. The one who drove them pulled 120 and swerved off a ledge. All of them died."

"Jesus," Jeremy muttered.

He heard those stories all the time. People getting drunk and crashing to their deaths. He'd even had a classmate in high school who ran over a little girl, instantly killing her, before crashing into a nearby tree and breaking his neck. Jeremy never understood that. He drank in abundance, but he never once thought about driving while drunk, not because he cared about his own well-being but

157

because he didn't want to kill other people by his irresponsibility.

Especially not children.

"And to think I had been angry with him because I thought he'd ghosted me," Dannie said. "I didn't realize how invested I was in the whole thing Caleb and I had until I saw the article. It really made me want to go back to using meds. And I came so close to it, too. So close. One of my former coworkers from the hospital was willing to sell the stuff to me for a cheap price. I still don't know how I managed to resist the temptation."

Jeremy scrunched his lips. Dannie's life was comprised of a series of obstacles and tests put there to trip her and see if she could get back on her feet. Just when she recovered from the first trial, the next one would knock her down and make her wonder if it was all even worth it. She would recover from that one, only to be ambushed by the next one.

For Jeremy, all those obstacles and tests were put together in one huge pile, a tsunami-sized bomb that would either destroy him entirely or leave him as a broken, shambling mess. He still wasn't sure which one of the two he belonged to.

"You quit your job after that?" Jeremy asked.

"No. But I did start looking for other opportunities. It wasn't just because of Caleb. As tragic as his death was, I got used to working there again pretty fast. It was empty at first, yes, but it's funny how the human brain can compensate for whenever we're missing something. The pay wasn't that great, so the whole thing was a boost for me to start looking for other jobs. And that's how I ended up here."

"Well, I hope you won't start looking for a new job if something happens to me tonight," Jeremy joked. The radio remained silent, so he added, "Sorry."

"It's all right. I guess I partly felt responsible for Caleb's death. I thought that maybe there was something I could have done to prevent it. But I'm not going to linger on regrets this time. I'm going to do everything in my power to get you out of there, Jeremy."

Dannie was seeking redemption. Another chance to prove that she wasn't the failure she considered herself to be. A reason to believe she could still make a difference in someone's life. That desire could prove to be deadly.

Jeremy inhaled deeply. "Listen, in case something does happen to me…"

"It won't."

"But if it does, don't blame yourself. There's really nothing you can do except contact the police. And that's out of your control. So, if something does happen tonight… don't beat yourself up."

Dannie hesitated before answering. "We'll discuss it later."

It was like she was mirroring his response earlier when she suggested they meet at the control tower. Jeremy decided not to call her out on her patronizing answer.

Just as he opened his mouth to say something, a giggle outside the door caught his attention.

CHAPTER 18

Jeremy's body tensed up, all his senses on edge. His hand clenched the scissors hard as his eyes fixed on the door.

Did he really hear that just now?

All his anxiety was suddenly back. The veil that had given him the false sense of safety for the past twenty minutes had fallen, revealing the disgusting reality nestled behind it.

Jeremy pointed the flashlight to the bottom of the door but detected no shadows underneath. Slowly, he bent his knees, placed a palm on the wall, and clambered up to his feet. His knees painlessly cracked from the lack of movement, and he cursed them for it. Then again, no need to be sneaky since the intruder already knew he was in here.

With his breath held in his lungs, he tip-toed to the door, his ears pulsating from the tension. He leaned his ear against the door, listening for any sounds outside.

Nothing but silence.

Jeremy prudently detached from the door and looked down at the keyhole. It was probably pitch black out there, but it wouldn't hurt to try to take a look.

He bent down, ignoring the creaking of his clothes. Since the keyhole was too low, he got down on one knee and aligned his sight with it. At first, he saw nothing. He blinked, waiting for his eyes to adjust. He pointed the flashlight under the door, hoping to illuminate at least a little bit of the hallway. If the flashlight helped, then the difference was negligible.

Jeremy stared, each second ticking away too slowly, the tension that swirled inside him growing.

Then, a patter of footsteps resounded just as a short shadow even darker than the hallway outside washed past the keyhole, a childish giggle following with it. Jeremy yelped and fell back, his rear hitting the floor. His heart rate went up as he stared at the keyhole. He hadn't registered how much his fingers hurt until he realized how firmly they clutched the scissors.

"Dannie? Are you there?" he asked.

"Always. What's wrong?"

"There's someone out there."

"Just stay inside the bathroom, okay? Is he trying to break in?"

"No, you don't understand. I don't think... I..." He gulped, the words refusing to leave his mouth. "I think it's Raymond."

There. He said it. Now it was too late to take back the words, and Dannie could think of him what she wanted.

"Raymond? Your son?"

"Yeah. Yeah."

"But Jeremy, you said he died."

"I know what I said!" Jeremy snapped. He was on his feet, his gaze transfixed on the door, cold sweat coating the nape of his neck. "I know what I said. I just... none of this makes any sense, but... It's him. I heard him. And I saw him. He just... he just ran past the... I saw him run past the bathroom just now, I swear it."

Silence lingered on the radio. He hated that moment of quiet that seemed to last forever because he couldn't tell what Dannie was thinking. She could be in awe at the paranormal activity surrounding the lighthouse, unable to find the right words. Or maybe she was thinking about how Jeremy was a lost cause, crazy, fit only for an insane asylum.

"Jeremy." Dannie sighed.

He heard it in her voice. She was trying to believe him, but he wasn't providing a good enough reason.

None of it mattered, really. As he stared at the door in front of him, his indecision somersaulted between staying inside the bathroom to avoid the intruder and opening the door and going after Raymond.

But then it hit him.

Raymond was out there. *Ray.* Ray, his son, was just outside the bathroom door. What the hell was he thinking, waiting to see what would happen? He had to find his son right now before he disappeared once again!

"I'm going out there to find him!" he said, but he didn't know why. Was he hoping for Dannie to knock a shred of reason into him? To tell him that, no, it wasn't Ray and it couldn't possibly be?

But it was. It was because he'd heard him.

Jeremy approached the door and pinched the lock. His hand jerked when the radio spoke up.

"Jeremy, I want you to listen to me, okay?" Dannie said, her voice stern, indicating she was about to say something that might sound like scolding. Jeremy's fingers squeezed the lock, itching to twist it. "Your son is dead. Okay?"

The words speared his gut. He'd known that, of course, and yet, for some reason, hearing it from Dannie made him feel like he'd heard it for the first time.

He didn't want to believe her. Something stirred inside him that hadn't stirred in a long, long time.

Hope.

He hated himself for it. He'd had that same dreadful feeling when the police officer had called him to inform him of his son's death. The entire ride to the school, Jeremy had refused to believe that it was Ray who got killed. He was sure that he would arrive at the school and see Ray safe and sound. Traumatized but alive. It would be someone else's kid who got killed.

Please, god, let it be that. I don't care if I burn in hell for thinking that way, but please, please, just keep my son safe, even if it means trading his life for someone else's, please.

But when he had arrived at the school, he realized that his prayers had fallen on deaf ears. He would never forget the relief on the other parents' faces as they wept and hugged their children. Their *living* children. He would never forget the hate and the jealousy he felt toward them.

Why should their kids get to survive, and not his? Was it just unlucky that his son was one of the victims? Or had a higher being orchestrated the whole thing, hand-picking the victims for that day?

He didn't want to go through that again. He didn't want to get his hopes up just to have them crushed once more. And yet, he couldn't stop that annoying hope from blossoming into something bigger, something that might transform into something beautiful or something equally grotesque.

He could have his son back. All his pains would be gone. Everything would be back to the way things were. Well, maybe not everything. Nadine would probably never go back to him, but he would have Ray back! He didn't want anything more than that.

Just the thought of hugging his son, seeing that he was alive and real made Jeremy's hands tremble with a feverish tremor.

"I'm going after him," he said as he twisted the lock.

CHAPTER 19

"Raymond?!" Jeremy opened the door wide and stepped outside, the cone of flashlight trembling violently.

An unnatural cold settled into his body, causing him to shake as if sick with a fever. The pattering of the rain was too loud.

"Jeremy, listen to me. I need you to go back inside the bathroom, please," Dannie said. "Please, just lock th... (khhh) and st... (khhh) ...ning un..."

Dannie's voice broke up and then went mute entirely. A part of Jeremy was grateful for that. He was not going to listen to her anymore. This was real. Ray was real, and she wasn't going to convince him otherwise. Not this time.

Jeremy scanned the hallway. No one was there. He strode into the living room. The place was a mess. The coffee table had been flipped over, the cups and mugs on it shattered into pieces that littered the floor. The window was broken, letting wind and rain invade the living room, drenching the couch and floor in front of them.

"Ray! Are you there?!" Jeremy called out, oblivious to the glass crunching under his boots.

Thunder cracked close by, causing Jeremy to jump. "Fuck," he hissed through his teeth. "Ray! Come on, son. Come out, all right?"

Lightning flashed outside. Jeremy gasped when his eyes fell on the tiny figure standing outside in the window. It was just for a split second before the flash was gone, engulfing the window in darkness once more. By the time Jeremy swiveled his flashlight to the window, the figure had left.

"Ray!" He ran after his son.

His boots kicked and crushed the glass on the floor as he poked his head through the window to scan the area. His eyes fell on the boyish silhouette in a red raincoat, running behind the lighthouse.

It was him. It was definitely him, no doubt about it. Jeremy would recognize that raincoat anywhere.

"Ray, wait!" Jeremy clambered on top of the broken window and hopped outside into the cold rain. He was full of enough energy to run for miles.

He dashed toward the pathway leading to the lighthouse. There he was. His son stood at the edge of the cliff, facing the ocean. Jeremy's stomach lurched. He broke into a sprint across the pathway, shouting Ray's name, but his voice was too muffled against the storm.

If Raymond heard him, he gave no indication of it because he continued standing stock still, his raincoat fluttering violently from the wind.

He's going to fall. Oh, god. I have to stop him before that happens.

He was rushing too fast and wasn't focused on the rocks below him. The next thing he knew, his foot slipped from under him, and he was plummeting headlong. The pain that radiated through his forehead when he hit the ground blurred his vision and caused his ears to buzz. Something warm tickled his nose, but even then, only one thought ran through his head: *I have to get to Ray.*

He looked up, to see the red silhouette of his son blurry against the night sky and spinning violently. Jeremy blinked to chase the blur away. Just as his vision started to clear up, the raincoated figure disappeared. It took Jeremy a moment to realize that Ray had jumped off the cliff.

"No!" he shouted, or at least, he thought he did, but the buzzing in his ears prevented him from hearing the words coming out of his mouth.

He planted his palms on the uneven surface. Just before pushing himself up, he noticed a droplet of red mixing in with the wet ground before being washed away by the downpour. He propelled himself forward, panic squeezing his throat.

It still wasn't too late. The cliff wasn't that tall. Ray could have hit the waters and was now treading them. Jeremy had to save him before he drowned. He just had to.

"Ray!" another pathetic shout escaped his mouth as he skidded to a halt near the edge of the cliff.

He looked over the ledge, completely forgetting about his acrophobia. He shouted his son's name once more as his eyes frantically scanned the roiling waves. Ray must have gone under, he must have gone—

His eyes fell on the red raincoat. It was hanging off the side of the cliff, snagged by one of the pointy rocks. But it wasn't a raincoat. It was just a piece of old, tattered, crimson cloth, soaked by the rain, battered by the wind.

No, it can't be. I saw him. I saw him.

But did you? Doctor Martelle asked. *Did you, really? All you saw was a silhouette.*

A silhouette that looked like a *boy*, Jeremy justified.

Did it? Did it really look like a boy?

That prompted Jeremy's brain to churn into an obsessive replaying of the scenes at the house. A giggle. There was a giggle. But it was so clipped that maybe… maybe it wasn't a giggle at all. It could have been anything else. Rubber screeching, wet boots shuffling…

But the figure at the window…

Just a trick of the light. Plus, you took your meds earlier. And there was an open whiskey bottle, so…

Jeremy grabbed his head, his fingernails digging into his skull. He couldn't think from the bullets of rain that crashed into his head.

He couldn't tell anymore what was real and what was not. He could swear he saw a little boy outside his window, running toward the lighthouse, standing near the edge of the cliff... but all of it could also be explained logically, and he hated that the most. He didn't want to think it was logical. He wanted to believe that Ray was here, alive, and waiting for his dad to find him.

Think, Jeremy. How could that possibly be Raymond? That boy looked no older than eight. Your son was fifteen when he died. That boy isn't Raymond. Snap the fuck out of it!

Jeremy hit his head with the palms of his hands in a desperate attempt to chase away the thoughts plaguing him. The red piece of cloth tore free from the cliff and gyrated through the air for a bit and twirled around itself, carried by the violent winds, before getting swallowed by the heavy waves below.

Then, like a flipped switch, his acrophobia was back at full force. Invisible weights pulled down on his neck toward the sharp cliffs. He backpedaled, away from the ledge, as the warmth was sucked out of his body at the realization that he could have fallen out of stupidity.

All of it was for nothing. Ray was still gone, and he was stuck outside in the rain.

"Fuck. Fuck, fuck, fuck!" Jeremy shouted.

The radio whirred and then stopped. "Dannie?" Jeremy pressed the PTT button. "Dannie, can you hear me?"

No response. He really needed to hear her voice right now.

"Shit!" He fought the urge to smash the radio on the ground.

His eyes shifted toward the house that now seemed so far away. The broken window was a gaping, black maw, open for anyone to enter. It didn't occur to Jeremy until then how stupid of him it was to put himself in such danger—again. And now he was a sitting duck, out in the open, unprotected by the house, which was exactly what the intruder wanted him to do.

If there even is an intruder.

He needed to get out of the rain, but going back to the house was not an option. Not anymore. The intruder might still be in there.

Just as he thought that, he caught a glimpse of something slinking away from the open window; a shadow that receded from the frame and merged with the darkness behind it. The intruder had been there the entire time, staring at Jeremy, mocking his every move.

There was no rage left to fuel Jeremy. The fear that was cooking in his gut all night long was finally reaching a boiling point, and with it, all his rational thinking evaporated, giving reins to the panic.

The crack of lightning was what spurred him to run. He rushed to the lighthouse door, his head turning to glance at the house every second or so, expecting to see the intruder taking menacing steps toward him with a knife raised above his head.

"Come on!" Jeremy fumbled with the keys until he found the right one and aimed at the keyhole.

The key sliding in was the most beautiful sensation ever. He turned the key, pushed the door open, and fell inside the lighthouse. He glimpsed one final time at the house—the house that no longer belonged to him, the house he was forced out of—and shut the door in front of him, making sure to lock it and double-check that it was locked.

The silence had never been as soothing as then. Jeremy stepped back. His heel caught on the stairs, and he fell on his rear. He didn't bother getting up. Not yet, anyway. He needed the break because his legs felt like they were mush.

He would climb as high up as he dared later on, but right now, he really needed a minute.

It wasn't the physical exertion that knocked him down so bad. It was the despair that grew from his chest and slowly enveloped his limbs and head. It was the hope that he'd had wilting away, decaying, turning into ashes.

He knew it. He knew Ray couldn't possibly be there, but he somehow convinced himself that he was. Why? Why did he think such a thing? It was so stupid, stupid, stupid of him. Now, the old wound was reopened, reminding him of all the pain he'd experienced the day he got that call from the police. Somehow, the agony was even more potent this time.

What did you think, Jeremy? That Raymond would just come back from the dead, say, "Hey Dad, I'm home. School was okay," and everything goes back to normal? Your son is dead, Jeremy. Raymond is dead. DEAD!

"Stop!" Jeremy's palms squeezed his temples as he rocked back and forth to get the voices out of his head. "Just fucking stop!"

He became vaguely aware of the pain in his forehead, in his palm, and his knee, but none of those things mattered. Physical pain, he could deal with. It was the voices in his head that were the real torture. It was the urge telling him to drink to forget about his problems that posed the biggest threat to him because he sometimes couldn't tell if the voice was a friend or a foe.

Just make it stop. Please make it stop, please, please.

The agony expanded until it was the only thing Jeremy knew about; until he was willing to do anything to make it go away.

The radio next to him crackled, a cut-off voice tearing from it before going mute. Jeremy wiped the rain and the blood and the tears from his face and fumbled for the radio so quickly that his shaking hands almost dropped it. "Dannie? Dannie, can you hear me? Are you there? Please, Dannie, respond!"

He desperately needed to hear her voice. He needed her to tell him everything was going to be okay, to tell him what to do in order to stay safe because he could no longer think straight. If she just responded to him, everything would be okay. Her voice would work like Xanax, and it would calm him down.

The radio whirred its wheezy sound, but Dannie's voice came through as imperceptible again; fragments of words that Jeremy couldn't understand because of the static.

"Dannie! Can you hear me? You're breaking up. Please, just try to say something."

But Dannie's response was another crackle, followed by silence. Jeremy continued trying to contact her, but the ensuing result was deafening stillness—not even the familiar crackle. Frustrated and unable to think from the throbbing pain in his forehead and palm, Jeremy stood up, hoping to be able to clear his head.

Okay. Calm down. One thing at a time.

His legs were a little steadier now. He descended the stairs into the basement and entered the bathroom. The first thing he did was take a look at himself in the mirror. The gaunt reflection that he'd seen back at the house was nothing compared to the ghost that stood now in front of him.

A diagonal gash adorned the middle of his forehead. It wasn't terribly deep but enough to keep the blood trickling down the middle of his nose, tickling it annoyingly. The palm of his hand had it the worst. The cut extended across the entire length of his palm, and it was much deeper.

Deep enough for stitches, he thought to himself as he flexed and extended his fingers, staring at the abundance of blood that refused to stop oozing out.

That one needed immediate medical attention. Jeremy opened the medicine cabinet and whipped out the first aid kit. He hesitated to pour alcohol on his palm, but it had to be done. He'd always seen heroes in action movies putting alcohol on their bullet wounds and wincing in pain, so he assumed it'd be painful, but he had no idea how painful it would be until the liquid touched his open wound.

Jeremy's hand spasmodically jerked as if electricity had stung it. He let out a groan at the burn. He gritted his teeth as he braced himself and spilled a little more on his hand. When he felt like he'd had enough, he put the bottle of alcohol aside, pressed a piece of gauze against the injury, and wrapped his hand in a bandage.

The injury on his forehead wasn't half as bad. He dabbed a little alcohol on it to clean off the blood and plastered a Band-Aid across it. Good enough until he received proper medical treatment.

Since his knee was painful, he rolled up his pants leg and inspected it, too. No visible wounds, but it looked a little swollen. He couldn't be sure if it was just his imagination, so he rolled up the other pants leg, too, and compared the knees.

The right one was definitely bigger, but Jeremy had no problem putting weight on it, which was good. The stairs would properly test if his knees were okay.

His entire body ached, but it felt good. The pain made him feel alive. Made him forget about the hallucinations outside.

Jeremy's eyes fell on the silent radio. He had to get in contact with Dannie. The comms room would help him with that.

Everything would be okay if he just reached the comms room.

CHAPTER 20

Jeremy hadn't realized he was hungry until his eyes fell on the crackers on the living quarters coffee table. They'd been sitting out for days, so they would probably be bland and sand-dry, but he didn't care. His stomach rumbled, and he needed some food.

He stuffed cracker after cracker into his mouth, his jaw working rapidly as it ground the food into powder and mush under his teeth. After the third one, swallowing became harder. He soldiered on until the entire package was gone.

His eyes fell on the floorboards with the secret booze stash. It would be perfect to wash down the crackers that clung to his teeth. He averted his gaze from it, determined not to let temptation lure him into the trap. He approached the sink and washed the food down with big gulps directly from the tap before wiping his mouth.

With a less empty stomach, he felt much better. He felt like his thoughts were clearing up somewhat, the panic kept at bay for the moment. His eyes fell on the "14 DEAD IN SCHOOL SHOOTING, SUSPECT SHOT BY POLICE" newspaper on the kitchen table. The only thing stopping him from crumpling the paper and throwing it in the trash was the fact that it was across the room, and he was too sluggish for such an explosive reaction.

Either way, it didn't matter. What mattered was reaching the communications room.

Jeremy climbed on, locking every door behind himself. If the intruder decided to go after him—and he was sure that he would—then Jeremy at least wanted to slow him down as much as possible. It couldn't be long until morning, right?

As he climbed the stairs, he replayed the entire night in his head, trying to determine how much time had passed. It felt like so many things had happened, but in reality, all those things occurred in a short span of time.

With that in mind, Jeremy was sure that the morning wasn't as close as he'd initially thought.

As soon as he burst into the comms room, his fingers located the light switch. By then, his knee was starting to become more painful. He turned the lights on and looked at the destroyed comms devices on the desk.

***

Smoke billowed from the electronics. Jeremy's nostrils only then registered the smell. Occasional sparks crackled from the electronics. The equipment was badly dented. Jeremy blinked, but this time, he was not met with that familiar feeling of surrealism.

After everything that had transpired tonight, something as innocent as destroyed communications devices struck no notes with Jeremy.

"Fuck," he muttered under his breath, his eyes darting across the communications desk, his brain actively looking for a way to salvage this situation.

He should have felt panic bloating his chest. He should have been angry. He should have felt *something*.

Instead, he found that he was oddly at peace with the problem in front of him. The comms devices had been destroyed, and really, what could he do about it? He couldn't fix them, so the only other thing left to do would be to despair and panic, but Jeremy didn't intend on doing that, so he simply stared.

What was he going to do now? Without a way to contact Dannie, he was really, truly stranded and alone.

It was the exhaustion that prevented him from feeling anything, he realized. Back when he first learned about the incident with Raymond, Jeremy spent days busying

176

himself at work with all sorts of stupid tasks and chores just to get his mind off things.

He was doing so good back then. He would have bouts of sadness during the day, but after crying his eyes out, he'd go back to work and continue focusing on it, instead. He would come home dead tired, unable to think about anything past slumping into bed, leaving the woes of tomorrow for tomorrow.

For a while, he thought he would be able to get through the pain that way—just work until the pain was completely gone. It would be like going to bed and not being aware of the eight hours that passed until breakfast.

Instead, all he did was delay the pain. When he got fired from work for his horrible performance, the pain of losing his child returned tenfold, and with nothing to keep him busy this time, Jeremy turned to heavy drinking.

Alcohol was yet another way to delay the pain, but he didn't care. The pain was too powerful for him to deal with it all at once.

Jeremy's shoulders drooped at the sight of the destroyed devices in front of him. He walked up to the desk, pulled out the chair, and plopped into the seat. His swollen knee thanked him for it. He put the radio on the desk, and like a school student who had spent the entire night cramming, he leaned across the desk and placed his forehead on his bent forearm, careful not to press the wounded part of the head.

He didn't care what happened next. He didn't care if the killer broke in and swung an axe at Jeremy. He just wanted to sleep. And not a five-minute nap or anything like that. No, he wanted a twelve-hour-long coma that would leave him feeling heavy and groggy and would be interrupted only by the rays of sunlight that would spear the room.

Peaceful thoughts wouldn't come, though. His mind raced to Raymond, to Nadine, to the times when the three of them were together and happy.

Jeremy especially cherished the private moments he and Ray had, the ones that Nadine didn't know about.

Like the time when Ray punched a bully in the face. That time, Jeremy had to explain to him that violence wasn't the answer and that, if he had a problem, he should come to his parents.

Or the time Jeremy found porn magazines tucked under Ray's bed. He had known that Nadine would find them sooner or later, and she would not react to that information as casually as Jeremy. So, Jeremy sat his son down and talked about the time when he, himself was a teen and hid magazines and VHS tapes from his parents.

Or the time Ray wanted to ask a girl who he liked out on a date but didn't know how to do it. Jeremy had given him some advice about it. Every private conversation ended with Jeremy saying, "Just don't tell Mom about it," except that last one, which ended with, "Feel free to ask Mom for additional tips."

He never knew that it would be his final advice to Ray.

Emily. That was the girl's name, Jeremy recalled. That happened sometime before the shooting, so Jeremy had no idea if Ray ever got the chance to ask the girl out. Either way, Emily was one of the victims, too. Jeremy rarely thought about her, but when he did, he couldn't help but wonder what his son's future would have been like.

That was the worst thing, perhaps.

Ray's life coming to an abrupt stop like that was like pausing a movie and never watching it to the end. Jeremy tried his best not to think about such gloomy topics, but he couldn't help but wonder sometimes what Ray would have been like.

178

He had liked video games, and he had talked about becoming a software engineer. He probably would have gone to a programming college. And after that? He'd come home every Christmas and Thanksgiving. He'd introduce a new girlfriend to his parents, and he'd talk about his college life. He'd finish college and get a job as a programmer, his girlfriend would soon become his wife, and then kids would be on the way. Pretty soon, Ray would be the younger version of Jeremy, and Jeremy would give the same advice to his son as his father had given him back when he and Nadine first got engaged.

And, what did Jeremy get instead?

A life without a future. A life without the people he loved and cared about. A life of staring at the bottom of a bottle, pondering what could have been.

"Jeremy?" Dannie called out, clear from the static.

Jeremy's head was immediately up, his hands grasping the radio and fumbling for the PTT button. "Dannie?! Can you hear me?!"

"Jeremy. Are you okay? I've been tr—" Dannie's voice turned into static.

"No, no, come on," Jeremy said, giving the radio a gentle whack. "You're breaking up, Dannie."

Another series of incoherent words came from Dannie's end, interrupted by the loud staticky noise.

"Shit. Shit!" Jeremy raised his hand to slam the palm on the desk, but then remembered that it was injured and bandaged. "Dannie, come on. Respond. Please, just… just say something. Please."

The static persisted, but then it stopped entirely, and Dannie's voice punctuated the air, clear as day, unhindered by any other noise. A single, atonal word that sent shivers running down Jeremy's spine. "Fourteen."

Jeremy never knew that one word like that one could drain the heat out of his limbs so fast. All he could do was

179

stare at the radio in silence as the word echoed in his head like a voice inside a spacious cave. The only explanation his frazzled mind could conjure up was that he had heard Dannie wrong.

As if hearing his conundrum, Dannie spoke up again, and this time, it left no room for doubt. "Fourteen people died that day."

Jeremy's breath hitched in his throat. The hand holding the radio trembled badly. He opened his mouth to say something, but how would one respond to that?

"Y-yes. Yeah. Fourteen people," was all he was able to mutter. Even if he knew what else to say, he wouldn't because he didn't trust his voice to not crack.

The radio went mute.

For a moment, Jeremy thought that the communication was scrambled again until Dannie spoke up, "Jeremy!" Her inflection was back to the familiar, worried one that Jeremy had grown accustomed to in the past couple of hours. "I think there's someone out here!"

Jeremy's heart leaped into his throat. The absurdity of that sentence made no sense; no sense at all. And yet, it did. Jeremy knew how much sense it made the moment he looked at the destroyed comms devices and the map plastered on the wall above—the map marking the lighthouse and the control tower.

The fear he felt in that moment far outweighed the fear he'd felt when his own life was in danger. The tables had turned, and now Dannie was the one who was in trouble.

"Dannie, talk to me. Who's out there? What do you see?"

"…need y… (khhh) sna… (khhh) it. Co… (khhh)" A loud skipping sound echoed, and then the radio went dead.

"Dannie? Are you still there? Can you hear me, Dannie?"

No response. Nothing. Not even static.

Somewhere outside, lightning struck the air, a flash bathing the window for a moment. Jeremy's eyes flitted to the window, his gaze fixated on the droplets of rain that refused to abate. What was the deal with this rain? Why wouldn't it stop?

For the first time that night, Jeremy could think with a clear head. He stood up, a frown forming on his face. "Dannie, I don't know if you can hear me, but I'm coming there. Okay? I'm coming!"

He didn't bother looking for weapons. There was no time for such meaningless things. He tucked the radio into his pocket and strode all the way down to the bottom of the lighthouse. He cursed himself for locking all the doors because he lost precious time fumbling with the keys.

Once he was back outside, he broke into a steady jog, away from the lighthouse, past the rocky pathway, past the still house that he'd lived in for the previous five months, and across the plains toward the tall trees that stretched over the dark horizon.

Toward the control tower.

CHAPTER 21

The area was so unfamiliar to him. He'd seen it every day for the past five months from the safety of the house, and he'd seen it when the company driver drove him up to the lighthouse, but he never once set foot on the grounds.

There had been no need to do it.

Jeremy didn't like walking so much anymore, and he especially hated walking on prairies that had no trees to provide shade from the unrelenting sun.

He'd been running for at least a few minutes. The trees that he ran toward were as distant as when he started, or so they seemed. Nestled somewhere behind that thicket was the control tower where Dannie was stationed. Jeremy had no idea how long it would take him to reach it, but he was determined to get there even if it took him all night long.

His right knee felt too tight, but at least there was no pain, which was good. His lungs burned from the running, and he had to slow his jog down for a while. Still, he was surprised by his own stamina. The last time he went for a casual jog in the park was over five years ago, and he barely managed to run a mile before running out of breath.

Now, he was breathlessly slogging toward the trees despite the protests of his body. He was sure that it had something to do with the scenario he was in. If he were to commit himself to running to the control tower just for fun, his dash probably would have slowed down to a meager walk by now. But Dannie's life was in danger, and he was sure that that was what gave him the necessary fuel.

He took only one look behind himself to see if anyone was following him—perhaps a hooded figure loping after him in a casual, Michael Myers style and still somehow managing to catch up. The prairie worked both to Jeremy's advantage and disadvantage.

The intruder wouldn't be able to sneak up on him, but at the same time, Jeremy would have nowhere to hide.

He couldn't shake the feeling that he was being watched from somewhere—somewhere very close by. When he scanned the surrounding area, though, he saw no one there. It must have been just his jumpy mind. Every time lightning exploded, Jeremy winced, wondering if the next one was going to fry him.

At the same time, it was beautiful. The white cracks that appeared momentarily above the trees illuminated the dark sky and the clouds that were otherwise invisible before merging once more with the darkness that veiled the horizon.

The thicket approached, the trees towering far above Jeremy, shrouding the whole area in an inky blackness. Jeremy still had his flashlight on him. He hurriedly whipped it out, the bright beam cutting through the dark and illuminating his path.

He took one final look over his shoulder and then stepped into the treeline.

***

Jeremy had forgotten just how dark forests could get at night. The artificial city lights and the moonlight above the unobscured sky provided a constant, comforting level of light that humans got used to. But under the canopies of the trees, away from any man-made city, with just a meager hand-sized tool as the only source of light, the darkness seemed thicker, more oppressive, as if trying to swallow the weak beam of the torch.

The thicket couldn't be long. He remembered carefully watching it when the driver drove him through the area five months ago. But then again, they were in a car, and those few minutes that it took to drive past the endless trees would take a lot longer on foot, trudging through the inhospitable terrain.

At least, the trees are blocking the rain a little bit, Jeremy thought to himself, determined to look at things positively just as Dannie had said. *Hold on, Dannie. Just, hold on. I'm on my way.*

What was he going to do once he arrived there? The only viable weapon he could use was the flashlight in his hand, and he wasn't sure how effective that would be. He tried not to think about that. He would cross that bridge when he got to it. One step at a time.

A sound gave Jeremy pause. He stopped dead in his tracks, listening, panting.

It took him a moment to realize that it was the radio in his pocket causing the broken-up static. Slices of words came through, not enough for Jeremy to understand what they were saying but enough to identify the voice as Dannie's.

He took the radio out and brought it to his mouth, "Dannie, can you hear me?"

More static. The communication should have been better by now. He was closer to the control tower after all. Then again, the trees might have been interfering. Coupled with the weather, it could scramble the communication badly.

"Dannie," Jeremy repeated.

"It's so lonely in here," Dannie said, the static gone. Her voice was laced with a sadness he hadn't heard her express up until then. "So lonely. I see him in my dreams, Jeremy. He's always running. I catch up to him, but when I spin him around, something's wrong with his face. It's not him. It's not our son."

Nadine.

Jeremy couldn't breathe. His hand almost dropped the radio. He had to lean on a nearby tree to stop himself from careening to the ground. He pressed the PTT button and then let it go. What was the point in talking? The voice he was hearing wasn't real.

For the first time that night, Jeremy considered something completely uncharacteristic of him, something so absurd and outlandish that even he, himself had trouble believing it.

"Ghosts," he found himself speaking aloud.

Even uttering that word caused the hairs on his forearms to prickle. *Ghosts.* Jeremy never once considered the paranormal to be true. He'd heard so many conflicted opinions about whether paranormal occurrences were real, and he always dismissed those theories as figments of imagination created by the human mind.

But now, stuck in the middle of the woods, at night, with a radio in his hand that spoke using his wife's voice, he knew, without a shred of doubt, that something was terribly *wrong* with this place.

Something existed in the lighthouse—no, on the entire land. Something malevolent that bid its time studying the visitors, their fears, their insecurities, and then used those against them, to drive them insane, to cause them to flee the lighthouse in the middle of the night, scared shitless.

Jeremy suppressed a peal of hysterical laughter.

He tucked the radio into his pocket and jackknifed into a confident gait forward.

Dannie needed his help.

***

The throbbing in Jeremy's hand had turned into a steady, dull pulsating. The bandages wrapped around his hand were soaked. He figured that there was no point in keeping the useless thing on his hand, but he refused to take it off because the gauze—no matter how wet—would at least protect the wound from opening deeper or wider, especially since he was so prone to reckless actions tonight.

The thicket stretched on and on like on a loop. Everything looked the same. The trees and the soaked moss-covered and leaf-covered ground, and the soggy twigs, and the darkness that perpetually went on for miles.

It was too late to turn back. Jeremy tunnel-visioned through the forest, afraid to turn around due to two reasons.

The first fear was that, if he turned to look behind himself, he would get completely disoriented and would end up going in circles. Perhaps that was already happening.

The second fear was that, if he did turn around, he would see nothing different. Just more trees and more darkness, the safety of the prairie and the beach and the lighthouse long gone, swallowed by the blackness.

If he continued going in one direction, he was bound to reach the other side—unless he was slowly and gradually being spun until he was facing the other direction without even realizing it.

It felt like diving into the pool. Back in college, he had taken swimming classes, and one of the tests was to dive the entire 25 yards-long lane and emerge on the other side. The problem was the college didn't provide them with goggles, so all the students were essentially blind underwater. Jeremy had ended up managing to swim the entire length, but when he surfaced, he noticed that he had gone a little to the right, which ended up being more than 25 yards.

The same could be happening now. The woods could be spinning him just as the pool did, and he might not even be aware of it. He chased those thoughts away, determined to reach Dannie before anything happened to her. He hoped he wasn't too late.

Not again.

I think there's someone out there, Dannie's words bounced inside his skull like a ping-pong ball, raising his dread and panic tenfold. Who? Who could it be? The same intruder that was messing around with Jeremy? The same *entity?*

Hold on, Dannie. Just hold him off until I arrive. I'll be there in a bit.

Just as he considered that, the trees grew sparser and sparser. Jeremy didn't know how, but he knew that this was the right way to go. He ran faster, the beam of his flashlight bobbing far up and gravitating down with each swing of his hand.

He was breathless, and a jolt of pain shot through his knee with each step, but it didn't matter. Just a little longer. A little longer.

And then, just like that, the trees disappeared, leaving Jeremy in a large, open, grassy area. A rim of trees surrounded the clearing, and in the center was the control tower.

CHAPTER 22

The tower itself was pretty much how Jeremy had envisioned it: a tall, metallic structure, not dissimilar to a fire lookout.

Jeremy's eyes flitted to the lit windows at the top. There, standing in one of the windows was a figure. Jeremy broke into a dash toward the stairs spiraling around the tower, leading up to the communications room. He clutched the flashlight firmly in his hand, prepared for the worst, ready to lunge at the intruder if needed.

He was going to protect Dannie; he didn't care what he needed to do.

His boots thudded loudly against the metallic steps. He swore the entire structure shook with each step he took. Step after step, he skipped up, his gaze fixated above him, fully expecting a figure to appear in front of him; a man around his age, as gaunt as him, a look of surprise on his face at the unlikely retaliation of the lighthouse keeper.

He didn't stop to look when he was at the top. His body worked on autopilot as he burst through the door and inside the comms room.

***

At the far end of the room sat a figure.

But it wasn't Dannie.

A burly person occupied the chair in front of the communications devices, facing away from Jeremy. He was somehow oblivious to Jeremy's presence, despite him bursting through the door like a cowboy.

Finally.

The intruder. The person who had been causing trouble to Jeremy this entire night. He thought he could feel a lopsided smile crooking his lips because he was going to enjoy getting revenge. At the same time, a twinge of unease crashed over him because one glance around the small room was enough to determine that Dannie wasn't there.

What had the intruder done to her? Where was she?

Jeremy's fingers squeezed the flashlight. He took a step forward and then stopped when the person on the other side of the room spoke up.

"Hello? Can anyone hear me?" his voice was shaky, petulant, riddled with obvious fear, as it should be.

"This is HQ. What's your status?" a tinny, straightforward voice spoke up.

"Oh, thank God!" The intruder let out a nervous chuckle. "I've been trying to contact you guys all night long. This is Lighthouse. Listen, I'm at the control tower. The lighthouse comms aren't working. I need you to send someone to pick me up ASAP!"

Jeremy froze, the crooked smile erased from his mouth. He couldn't will himself to move, no matter how hard he tried.

"Repeat that last, Lighthouse," the person from HQ said in a reticent tone.

"I'm at the old control tower! I had to get away from the lighthouse. Something's wrong with it. Someone... someone's there, and they've been messing with me all night long! Please, please, just send someone!"

Jeremy's stomach lurched at those words. He opened his mouth, but his throat was too closed up for him to say anything, at least for a moment. Gradually, the constriction allayed, and the flurry of words that had been stuck in his throat finally left his mouth.

"What the hell do you think you're doing?! Where's Dannie?! What did you do to her?! Where is she?!"

The loud words abraded his throat. Spittle flew from his mouth. And yet, despite the indignation that enveloped him like a python, Jeremy's feet refused to cooperate and step forward.

He wanted to strangle the intruder for lying to HQ like that. He wanted to bash his head in with the butt of the flashlight over and over until his skull was a bloody, soupy mess. But still, he couldn't move.

"Ten-four, Lighthouse. The police are on their way. Are you in immediate danger?" the tinny voice asked.

"No, not yet. At least I think not." The person in the chair leaned forward to look out the window then swiveled his head left and right, enough for Jeremy to catch a glimpse of his chubby cheeks. He was around Jeremy's age, from what he could tell.

Jeremy hissed, his hands trembling from how hard he was squeezing them into fists.

"What kind of danger are you in, Lighthouse?" HQ asked.

"I don't know! I… It could be a stalker or something. He's been messing with me all night long. But maybe, it's… it's…"

"Where's Dannie?!" Jeremy shouted, panic swelling in his chest.

But the intruder refused to look at Jeremy. He refused to acknowledge Jeremy's presence, and that only caused the panic that held tightly on to Jeremy to sink its claws deeper into his skin.

Just then, Jeremy's radio crackled to life. Jeremy looked down at the radio in his pocket. It produced the familiar *khhh*, and then Dannie's voice draped the air. "You know where I am, Jeremy."

Jeremy whipped out the radio with trembling hands. For the first time that night, he was afraid to press the PTT button. He was afraid to talk to Dannie because he knew he wouldn't like what she would tell him. And still, like driftwood carried by the ocean waves, he pressed the button because it was the only thing to do.

"Wha… what are… Dannie, what's going on?"

"You know what's going on, Jeremy. You've known all along what's going on."

"I… I don't understand. I don't understand. I just don't understand any of this." Jeremy grabbed his head to stop the dizziness that suddenly overcame him.

"Think back, Jeremy. Think really hard. I need you to do that," Dannie said.

"No, no, no. I can't. I… I don't understand. I can't." Tears trickled down his face. Snot ran from his nose as he whacked his head with the palm of his hand.

"I need you to think back, Jeremy. Remember. Can you do that?"

"No, no. What? Think back to when? I don't understand what you're saying. You're not making any sense."

Dannie let out a deep sigh, equivalent to that of a disappointed parent. Jeremy knew because he used to sigh just like that when Raymond did something to get into trouble. "I'm going to help you, okay? Because you have to remember."

Jeremy shook his head. He wasn't sure if he wanted to remember. But Dannie forced him to remember nonetheless.

"Fourteen dead in school shooting—suspect shot by police." Dannie proclaimed in a theatrical, reading tone, like a news reporter. The words sliced through the air like a knife through butter. Jeremy felt his legs cutting off. Nausea squeezed his stomach. Dannie gave Jeremy no time to recuperate. She continued with the same, robotic tone as if reading off a paper, which she might as well have been doing. "At least twelve teenagers and two teachers were killed in the May 21st shooting at Jackson High School.

191

The alleged gunman—identified by the authorities as 15-year-old Raymond Hefner—was killed by law enforcement at the scene."

Jeremy's ears buzzed. His knees wobbled, and he barely stood on his feet. His vision grew dark. Dannie's reading continued, but it was a muffled murmur. The image before Jeremy spun and somersaulted. He didn't know when he fell on all fours. He barely even registered that he was retching, no vomit coming out of his mouth, not even those dry crackers that he had wolfed down earlier.

Transparent droplets fell from his eyes on the floor below him. He squeezed his eyes shut to get the tears out. He couldn't breathe. His arms shook like branches in the wind.

He remembered everything now. Every nasty detail that he had buried deep within his subconscious mind, hoping never to extract them again. Now they were back, like a volcano eruption, their potency immeasurable. He remembered *everything*.

Coming to the school to see what was going on, only to be told by the police that his son had gone on a killing spree. Only weeks later would psychiatric experts determine that Raymond had finally snapped due to all the bullying in school.

A stupid, stupid, *stupid* reason to go on a rampage and kill fourteen innocent people, twelve of which were teens. A tragedy that could have been prevented if only Jeremy and Nadine didn't have their noses buried in their jobs all the time. If only Jeremy had stopped once in a while to talk—really talk—to his son, and not give all the bullshit template advice, maybe things would have been different.

Maybe he would have noticed the pain peeking between the cracks. Maybe he would have been able to give Ray some words of assurance, tell him things would not always be that bad. Who cares if your classmates don't like you? Who cares if the girl you like said no when you asked her out?

Emily. She had been the final straw for Ray. When he'd asked her out, she didn't just say no. She made sure to let everyone in the school know about it. Jeremy was sure that the bullies couldn't wait to publicly humiliate Raymond.

Jeremy had only found out about it weeks after the massacre. He was too busy with his stupid work to notice his son retreating and becoming a recluse. After years of being bullied, he'd had enough.

He'd dug up Jeremy's guns, put them in the car, drove to school, and...

At moments, at very tiny intervals, Jeremy found himself feeling glad that at least Ray's bullies were dead. It was their fault that Ray did what he did. If they just accepted his son for who he was...

Just as quickly as those horrible thoughts would come to Jeremy, he would push them down because those teens, even if they were bullies... they were still someone's children, and they didn't deserve to die.

While all the families of the victims mourned the loss of their children, Jeremy and Nadine had to mourn another extra thing: the knowledge that their son was an indiscriminate murderer and that they would carry the blood of those victims on their hands for the rest of their lives.

While the families of the victims received thoughts and prayers and financial help, Jeremy and Nadine received threats, and Raymond was demonized by the media as a monster. They were wrong, Jeremy kept trying to tell them. Raymond was just misunderstood. Troubled.

But they were right.

He *was* a monster, and every time an unflattering picture of Raymond popped up on the news next to the headline reminding the readers of the atrocity he had committed, Jeremy would see it.

He couldn't take being bullied, so he opted to bring others down with him. Even in death, he would continue to bring pain to those families, year after year after year, a constant reminder that one person singlehandedly destroyed fourteen lives.

All Jeremy wanted to do after the shooting was to mourn his son's death. But he couldn't do it. Not publicly and not even in the privacy of his house with Nadine. They both thought the same thing: They hated and loved Raymond just as they hated and loved each other—and themselves.

It was the most conflicting feeling Jeremy had ever felt. Raymond was a monster, but he was still Jeremy's son.

"Jeremy," Dannie said, the reading tone replaced by a somber one. "I'm sorry."

Jeremy looked to the right. The radio was on the floor next to him. He didn't remember when he had put it there. With one gelatinous hand, he reached toward the radio, reeled it in, and pressed the PTT button. It took all the strength in his body to do so.

"You… y-you knew all along, di-didn't you?" he asked through a sobbing hiccup.

"I didn't. But you did. I was here just to remind you."

Jeremy let out a chuckle. He laughed until that laughter morphed back to weeping. "Then you're not really here, are you? It's just me and… and…" He looked up at the intruder in the chair. "Just me and him."

"No. Not you and him, Jeremy," Dannie coldly said.

"Lighthouse, repeat. What is the nature of the danger?" the tinny voice of HQ asked.

"I think…" the intruder said. "I think it's a ghost."
194

Pain jolted through Jeremy's skull. He closed his eyes and gritted his teeth as images ran through his head.

Images of him standing on the walkway while the rain pattered around him and lightning occasionally flashed in the distance. The violent waves stood far below him.

He contemplated jumping down there. The pain would be erased just like that. Everything would be erased, and sweet nothingness would embrace Jeremy—or whatever the afterlife offered. Hell, rebirth, ceasing to exist—it didn't matter.

All that mattered was getting rid of the pain.

Jeremy ducked under the railing until he was on the other side, hanging over the edge of the walkway. His hands gripped the metal bars behind him. His toes poked over the ledge, his heels the only foothold he had. He was staring down at the waves that grew more violent and hungry in anticipation.

And then...

He let go.

The fall was a lot more peaceful than he thought it would be.

No screaming.

No second thoughts.

No fear.

Just the eagerness for the approaching waves to embrace him.

"Dannie?" he asked, his voice wobbly.

"Yes, Jer?" Dannie asked solicitously.

Jer.

Strangely, he'd learned to love that nickname again over the course of the last few hours.

"Thank you," he said.

EPILOGUE

"A ghost?" HQ asked.

Orlando could detect mockery in the radio person's voice. He pretended not to hear that between-the-lines snicker as he leaned closer to the microphone. "Yes. Those stories that the lighthouse is haunted... they're all true. And I've seen them. I've seen the—"

A dull sound behind him caused him to snap around. The door of the control tower was open. When had that happened? Orlando gasped, scanning his surroundings for anything unusual.

But he wouldn't see anything; he already knew that much. The stalker that he was up against was invisible. Orlando's hand traced his collarbone, squeezing the cross that hung around his neck. Perhaps it was his mother's prayers that kept him alive all night long, especially when things started going crazy back at the house.

"Hello? Is somebody there?" he asked, his voice boyish and scared.

Nothing.

He quickly broke into a gait to close the door, and—

His foot kicked something on the floor. His gaze gravitated to the object, and he realized that it was the radio that had gone missing from the comms room in the lighthouse earlier that day. "Huh."

Orlando bent down to pick it up. It was wet from the rain but still functional, from what he could tell.

"Lighthouse, do you copy?" HQ's voice boomed from the control panel behind him.

Orlando straightened his back and gave his surroundings another once over. He only just then realized that the pattering of the rain had stopped. The chirping of the birds replaced the downpour. When he turned around, the crimson sun was shyly poking its head above the treetops, chasing away the blackness shrouding the sky.

Dawn was here.

A new day.

With it, the threat that had plagued Orlando all night long seemed to disperse. He couldn't tell how, but he felt safe once more, for the time being. The lighthouse would still have its quirks from time to time, but that was normal.

After all, the place was haunted. Nothing a few candles and crosses wouldn't fix.

"Lighthouse, respond," HQ insisted.

Orlando clipped the radio to his belt and walked up to the control panel. "I copy. I'm heading back to the lighthouse. I'll wait for the cops there."

"Ten-four, Lighthouse. Stay safe out there."

Orlando stretched, gazing out into the forest outside. It was so peaceful out here. That's why he took up the job in the first place.

As if he had jinxed it, a loud *khh* erupted from his belt. Orlando looked down, his eyes fixed on the radio. For a moment there, he thought he heard something other than the static. Something that sounded like a gruff voice chuckling.

Orlando exited the control tower, determined to finish his final month at the lighthouse, haunted or not.

THE END

ABOUT THE AUTHOR

Boris Bacic (spelled Bačić in his native tongue) was born in 1990 in Serbia, in a small Northern town called Subotica.

As a kid, he developed a passion for writing and drawing because it allowed him to dive into a world of his own. When he started going to high school, he stopped writing for a while and focused on fitness in hopes of becoming a police officer (or a soldier).

After serving in the army, he worked as a fitness coach for a few years before becoming interested in Creepypastas (short, scary stories found on the internet). He spent a long time reading horror stories and listening to Creepypasta narrations before deciding to post his own story on Reddit's Nosleep forum. He immediately got tons of recognition and praise from the frequent readers and had his stories narrated by prominent Youtubers – some of which include MrCreepypasta, MrCreeps, DarkSomnium, DrCreepen, etc. – translated into various languages, and his most popular Nosleep series, **Tales of a Security Guard**, is currently being made into a video game and short film.

Boris published his first book in 2019, titled **Scary Stories With B.B.**, and has since become an award-winning author with titles like **Apartment 401**, **Camp Firwood**, and **It Came With The Crash**. He has also reached #1 Bestseller in multiple categories on Amazon.

In his free time, he enjoys going to the gym, reading books, playing video games, exploring topics for his next book project, and occasionally, going to escape rooms.

Message from the author:

Want to get in touch with me? Shoot me an email at:
authorborisbacic@gmail.com
I always love hearing from my readers.
BB

FINAL NOTES

Thank you for reading my book. If you enjoyed it, I would appreciate it if you left a review on the **Amazon Product page**. Your reviews help small-time authors like me grow and allow us to continue expanding our careers and bring you – the readers – more stories like these.

More From The Author

BOOKS IN THE HAUNTED PLACES SERIES

BOOK 1: APARTMENT 401

There's something wrong with apartment 401…

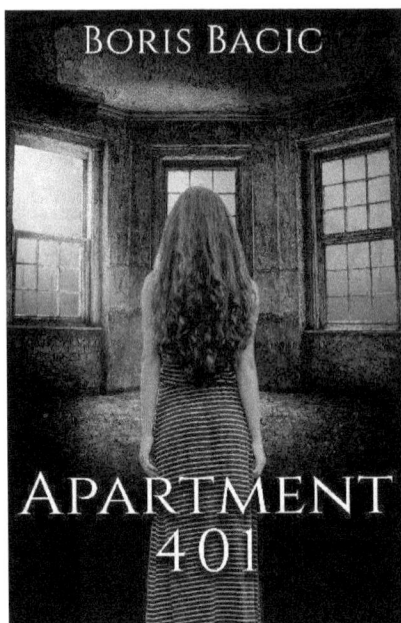

BOOK 2: THE DOOR

There's a locked door in Nathan's new apartment. At night, it opens.

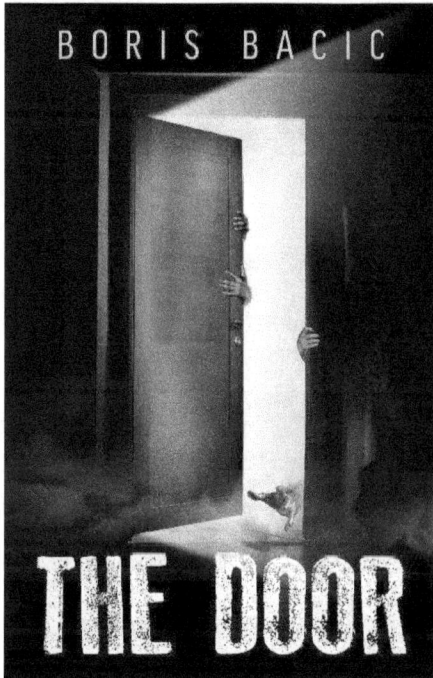

BOOK 3: HER HOME

Even with her mother in a coma, the house is anything but quiet.

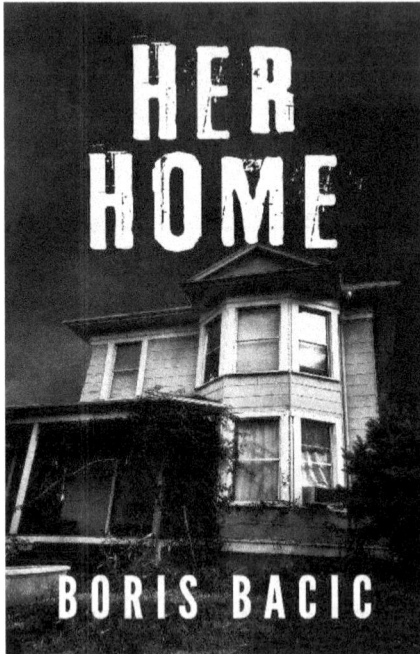

BOOK 4: YOKAI ISLAND

If you hear whistling, stop moving immediately.

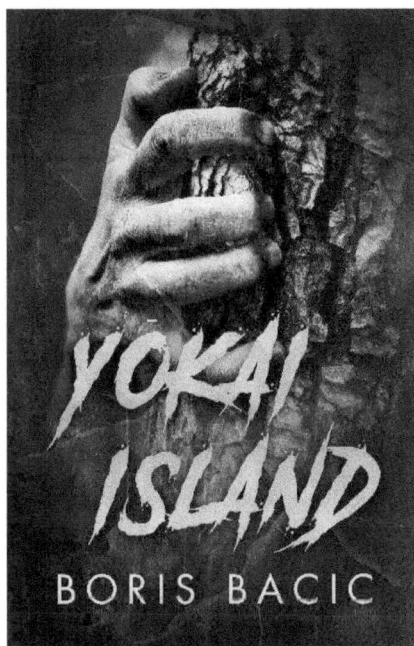

BOOK 5: SINISTER MELODY

If you hear the music, you're as good as dead.

Lightning Source UK Ltd.
Milton Keynes UK
UKHW010956080223
416610UK00015B/1706